The Captain's Bluestocking Mistress

ERICA RIDLEY

Four left for war…
Only three made it home.

Chapter One

March 1816
London, England

UNDER NORMAL CIRCUMSTANCES, Miss Jane Downing would have been eager to alight from a chilly carriage and rush indoors for a welcome respite from the brutal winter. The exquisite building in front of the long line of coaches was none other than the Theatre Royal. The Duke of Ravenwood himself had loaned them his magnificent box for the occasion.

Most debutantes—most *anyone*, for that matter—would have been in raptures at such an opportunity.

Jane was not.

She was old enough to be more properly labeled a spinster than a debutante, if anyone chanced to glance her way long enough to label her anything at all. She sighed. Unlikely. After all, the princely theatre box hadn't been loaned to *her*. She was no one.

But because even invisible old maids couldn't gallivant about unchaperoned, her best friend Grace and her husband the Earl of Carlisle (to whom the box had been gifted) had driven in the opposite direction of the opera house in order to collect Jane and return to Covent Garden in time for the performance. All she could do was keep a smile on her face and do her best to be charming.

The ignominy of her inconvenienced friends wasn't why Jane wished she were elsewhere, however. Those were everyday trials. And these *were* her friends.

Grace reached across the small interior to squeeze Jane's hands as the wheels of the coach inched forward in the queue to the theatre. "Thank you ever so much for joining us. This is my first opera, and I am delighted to be sharing the night with all of my favorite people."

Jane gave Grace's hands an answering squeeze. In situations like these, the best thing to do was to lie through one's teeth. "I'm thrilled to be here. Thank you for inviting me."

She folded her hands back into her lap and wished for something else to say to break the renewed silence. She was adept at conversation when she was speaking privately with someone she was comfortable with. But she and Grace weren't alone in the coach. Grace's mother, Mrs. Clara Halton, sat to Jane's left, gazing lovingly across the carriage toward her daughter. Lord

Carlisle, of course, sat next to his wife, watching her as if the moon and stars paled next to her beauty.

Jane would *kill* to have a man look at her like that. Just. Once.

Lord Carlisle hadn't stopped looking at Grace like that. Not since the moment he'd first caught sight of her. Jane should know. She'd seen it happen. From her eternal vantage point among the spinsters and the shadows, she observed everything. Other people laughing, dancing. Falling in love.

Yet spending the entire evening with a newly wed, obviously besotted couple wasn't what had her biting her lip and cursing her jittery leg. Jane was delighted for her friends. She loved spending time with them.

She hated being out in Society. No—she hated being *invisible* in Society.

Her friends wouldn't understand. Before Grace had ensnared an earl and become his countess, back when she'd been penniless, gauche, and *persona non grata* for being an upstart American, she'd still caught everyone's eye. After all, Grace was beautiful. With her white skin, black hair, and sparkling emerald eyes, she easily attracted the attention of men and women alike.

Jane couldn't even attract mosquitoes.

It wasn't because she was plain. Many plain women managed to be popular and find husbands. Not Jane. In four-and-twenty years, she'd only twice been invited to dance.

Her dreams of finding someone were just that. Dreams. She smoothed out her skirts. It wasn't the few extra pounds on her frame, or that she was an unrepentant bluestocking. Her life-long curse was the unfortunate fact of being utterly, absolutely, one hundred percent… forgettable.

Her head began to ache as the carriage wheels inched her ever closer to a long night of being ignored and misremembered.

Even with all this snow and the serpentine trail of coaches, she and her companions would have plenty of time to mingle by the refreshments before taking their seats.

Jane slumped against the squab. Mingling was horrid. Mingling was standing still in a sea of faces that never once turned in her direction.

She turned her gaze toward the street and sat up straighter. A cluster of well-dressed gentlemen flocked toward a row of women strolling toward the theatre in stunning, bright-colored gowns. *Courtesans*. She stared out the window, fascinated. These men were hunting their next mistresses.

Her nostrils flared as the men danced attendance upon the demimondaines. Some of the Cyprians were gorgeous and some were ghastly, but each of them would receive more male attention in one night than Jane would in her entire life.

How ironic that the same gentlemen who had never thought to ask Jane to dance would gladly spend exorbitant sums of money in exchange for an hour in the company of a woman with less education and a worse reputation than she had.

What must it be like to be one of them? These weren't desperate, gin-addicted whores in some bawdy house, forced to accept every brute with a penny. These women were elegant and expensive. They could select their lovers as they pleased.

Jane tilted her head. If she could have any man she wished, who would it be?

A dark, hard-as-granite officer with haunted blue eyes sprang instantly to mind. Captain Xavier Grey.

Heat pricked her cheeks. Of course he sprang to mind. He was all the *ton* spoke about, and one of the earl's dearest friends. He had always caught Jane's eye. Years before, when he was merely Mr. Grey, he had still been handsome and confident and the last person on earth who might notice the mooning gaze of a soon-to-be spinster. And then he'd left for war.

Three years later, he'd become a hollow husk of a man, beautiful and broken. He'd remained locked inside his head until Lord Carlisle had rescued the captain from—well, wherever he'd been—and returned him to England, determined to give him back some life.

The last time she'd seen the captain was over
a month ago, the night Grace and Lord Carlisle
had been compromised into marriage. He had
seemed so... defeated. The *ton* was in full agree-
ment that Captain Grey had miraculously
awoken from his fugue that very night, but Jane
held a private opinion.

For him to "awaken" implied he'd been in a
state of arrested consciousness, and she didn't
believe that was the case at all. Every time she'd
glimpsed him, his eyes had been too tempestuous
to imagine him unaware of the world about him.
He just no longer wished to be part of it.

Jane wrapped her arms about her chest and
tried to put him out of her mind.

The time to obsess over a strong, silent soldier with dark, haunted eyes was five hours from
now, when she was alone in bed with her
thoughts. Right now, she needed to focus on being a good friend.

She gave her companions her sunniest smile.
"How go the renovations on Carlisle House?"

Grace's eyes lit up. "'Tis only been a week
since the wedding, so we haven't purchased
much—aside from furnishings for my mother's
chambers, of course." She sent a fond glance toward her mother, then touched her fingers to
Lord Carlisle's chest. "I don't care about chandeliers and fancy gowns. What we have is more
than enough. I want Oliver to spend every penny
on his tenants before restoring the estate."

"And I don't want *you* to lack a single comfort," Lord Carlisle responded gruffly as he pressed a gentle kiss to the top of his wife's hair.

Wasn't that adorable? Jane clenched her teeth behind her smile. She wasn't jealous in the slightest.

No. This was going to be a splendid evening. She was fortunate to have been invited. This opera was one of her favorites.

She pasted the smile back on her face.

"What are your duties while Lord Carlisle handles his affairs?" she asked her friend. "I imagine managing such a large household must be a challenge."

Grace shook her head. "I thought so at first, but they don't require much direction from me. Most of the staff has been working there since Oliver was a child. What I truly wish we had is some entertainment for Mama. The library is empty, and—"

Lord Carlisle swung his head sharply in her direction. "I shall order a dozen titles as soon as the tenants' roofs have been repaired."

Her chin jutted forward. "Absolutely not. You have other duties a hundred times more important than travel tomes and gothic novels. I refuse to—"

"*I* have books," Jane interjected before the fight could continue. "I can lend..." She coughed into her gloved fist. No. She could do better than that. These people counted their shillings, and she loved them dearly. "…that is, *give* you as many history tomes and gothic novels as you might like."

Lord Carlisle's voice hardened. "We couldn't possibly."

Jane made a self-deprecating gesture. "Your wife's best friend is a bluestocking with more books than sense. You might as well get *something* out of the association."

Even if it killed her. She rubbed her suddenly chilled arms. Just the thought of losing any part of her collection left her empty.

Every book, every story, was dear to her heart. For long, lonely weeks at a time, the only conversation she heard was the dialogue printed within those pages—well, that and the gentle prodding of her brother's servants if she missed a meal. Books kept her company so often that she had a fair quantity memorized. *Mansfield Park.* *Waverley. Guy Mannering.* Her throat convulsed. Of course she would relinquish her dearest possessions to Grace and her mother.

That's what friends did.

Grace reached across the carriage to squeeze Jane's hand again. "You are the kindest woman who ever lived. I will accept a loan, but not a gift. We shall return your books as quickly as we can read them."

Some of the tightness left Jane's shoulders. "As you please."

The carriage jerked to a stop. Lord Carlisle and Mrs. Halton exchanged pleased smiles. Grace clapped her hands in excitement.

Jane concentrated on making it through the night with her pride intact.

Lord Carlisle helped his wife from the carriage, then his mother-in-law. When it was Jane's turn to alight, she rallied her courage and forced herself up from the squab. It was just a Society event. She would survive.

Once on Bow Street, they bent their heads against the bitter wind and dashed into the theatre lobby. Warmth enveloped them. To the others, the heat from the fireplace might have been welcome, but to Jane, it was her cue that she had officially entered Hell. Throngs of fashionable faces crowded them at once.

"Lord Carlisle! Lady Carlisle!"

"You look radiant, Lady Carlisle! Lovely to meet you, Mrs. Halton!"

"I fancy you want your grays back, Carlisle. Their price has doubled, I daresay!"

"*Please* say you'll come to our dinner party next month, Lady Carlisle."

"Ravishing bride, Carlisle. I hear the mother's a widow?"

"Congratulations on your nuptials, Lady Carlisle. Is this stunning woman your mother?"

"She is!" Grace chirped, radiant as a new countess. "Your Grace, I present Mrs. Halton. Mama, this is His Grace, the Duke of Lambley."

A firm grip latched onto Jane's wrist and yanked her to Grace's side. "And this is Miss Downing, my best friend. She's as brilliant as she is beautiful."

The duke bent over Jane's fingers. "In that case, I am very pleased to meet you."

"As am I." She refrained from mentioning they'd met on at least ten prior occasions. It wasn't his fault. Rakes couldn't be expected to recall the names of all the ladies they'd tupped, much less the face of lowly wallflower.

"Grace!" squealed a happy female voice. "That is, *Lady Carlisle*. Do you *adore* being a countess?"

"I definitely adore my earl," Grace answered with a laugh. "Matilda, this is my friend Miss Downing. Jane, I'd like you to meet Miss Kingsley."

It seemed churlish to say, *I met her when we had our come-out on the same evening, then again when her cousin disappeared at a musicale and Miss Kingsley needed someone to turn the pages, then again when the ladies' club collected embroidered handkerchiefs for charity*, so Jane just sighed and said, "How do you do?"

As she always, always did.

Emptiness yawned inside of her. Jane wasn't just a fixture in Society—she *was* a fixture. No more memorable than a carpet or a bellpull.

Grace looped her arm through Jane's and turned her toward one of the young men. "This is my best friend, Miss Downing. Jane, this is Mr. Fairfax."

Another familiar face.

He touched his lips to the back of Jane's gloved hand. "Don't believe everything they write about me in the scandal sheets."

She smiled brightly. "So you're *not* an incurable rogue addicted to gaming hells and pricy brothels?"

Grace groaned into her hands.

Jane blinked back at her innocently.

As expected, Mr. Fairfax wasn't listening. His gaze had already been caught by a young lady in an emerald dress, and he was even now disappearing into the crowd without remembering to say good-bye.

Grace cast Jane a look, but before she could say a word of chastisement she was once again surrounded by well-wishers. "Oh, of course, Lady Grenville! I would love for you to meet my mother. Mama, this is …"

Jane stepped back into the shadows. She supposed the positive aspect to never being recalled was that she could get away with some truly outlandish behavior. Mr. Fairfax hadn't been insulted. He'd already forgotten her.

She let the voices fade to a distant buzz. Her ability to ignore the outside world and live inside her head was key to getting through each boring, endless day. When at home, it let her escape into her books. And when at the Theatre Royal…

Well, living inside her head was better than being introduced to the same blank faces time and again.

Others might not mind. Her brother, Isaac, *preferred* being invisible. He was boring on purpose, just to keep his name off the Marriage Mart's most wanted list. He cherished his solitude.

Jane was the opposite. She often said the most outrageous things she could think of in the hopes of seeing awareness flash for just one second in someone else's eyes, but it never, ever happened. If there was a boring, harmless way to interpret her boldest insults or double entendres, that's precisely how her remarks would be taken—and then promptly forgotten. It was as though High Society suffered from total Jane Amnesia. *Janenesia*.

"Ladies." Lord Carlisle proffered one arm to his wife and the other arm to her mother. "It's time to take our seats."

Jane trailed in their wake.

It wasn't that her friends had forgotten her. Lord Carlisle possessed two arms and was escorting three women. Besides, Jane was used to walking unnoticed in other people's shadows.

When she was younger, she'd thought perhaps her stride was the problem. That maybe she'd copied so much of Isaac's careful boringness that her very walk made her invisible.

Easy enough to correct! She'd tried strutting like a peacock. Shimmying like a demimondaine. Swaggering like a dandy. Once, she'd shuffled ploddingly behind her brother with her mouth hanging open as if she were the walking dead intent on eating him alive. At the annual Sheffield Christmastide ball. In front of hundreds of witnesses. At the very least, she'd expected to gain a horrid-but-catchy nickname, like *Lady Automaton* or even *That-Poor-Miss-Downing-What-Do-You-Suppose-Is-Wrong-With-Her?*

Nothing. Not a blink. Complete Janenesia.

Lord Carlisle paused in front of Ravenwood's opera box and held back the curtain. Mrs. Halton slipped inside first, followed immediately by Grace. Just as Jane moved forward, Lord Carlisle stepped in behind his wife. The curtain didn't *precisely* fall on Jane's head. She pushed the curtain aside and hurried inside as quickly as possible. The box was dim, but sumptuous. She pushed a few more pins into her displaced curls and settled into an empty seat.

Of course Carlisle wished to sit next to his wife. They were newly wed. And Jane was a never-will. Even if she could somehow command a man's attention, with what would she keep it? Her brain was a mark against her, and as for her alleged beauty... Her own papa had always said she was quite pretty—for a plump girl.

Although the current high-waisted fashions did nothing to hide her plumpness, the billowing tubular midsection gave *all* women a rounder midsection, so at least she wasn't the only young lady thus afflicted. Just the only undesirable one.

The audience rumbled excitedly as the thick red curtain began to part onstage.

Grace leaned into her husband, her brow furrowed. "He's not coming?"

Lord Carlisle slipped her hand in his. "He'll be here. He would never break his word."

Jane kept her voice hushed as she turned toward them. "*Who* won't break his word?"

"An old friend," Carlisle murmured at the same moment Grace said, "Captain Grey."

Chapter Two

HEAT RACED UP JANE'S CHEEKS. Captain Grey? Was joining them *here?*

Her entire body was blushing, just at the sound of his name. And the reminder of the rather lurid thoughts she had about him every time she closed her eyes.

She couldn't move a muscle. Heaven help her, she could barely even *think*. This was a disaster.

The last thing this evening needed was the object of her fantasies to sit right beside her and remain unaware of her existence. She'd rather return home now, before complete and utter humiliation had a chance to rear its ugly head.

"How do you know he's coming?" she asked breathlessly.

"Because he said so." Lord Carlisle lifted his wife's fingers to his lips. "I told him it would please Grace if he would join us at least once before removing to Essex."

"He's... leaving?"

Grace nodded. "Tomorrow. He has a little cottage a couple miles past Chelmsford and he plans to stay there the rest of the Season."

"Or perhaps forever." Carlisle's jaw tightened. "Xavier thinks he may never be ready for Polite Society. He may be right."

Jane swallowed hard. Of course the dark and dangerous man of her dreams planned to disappear from Society forever after tonight. What did she expect?

The curtain to the private box flung open. There, silhouetted by the chandeliers in the corridor, stood the infamous Captain Grey… and a very imperious usher.

A wry smile quirked the corner of Captain Grey's lips. "I'm afraid my good man here couldn't quite credit that I was welcome in the Duke of Ravenwood's box. Shall I go?"

Lord Carlisle sprang to his feet. "Of course you're welcome! Come, sit. I believe you know everyone present?" He turned toward the usher. "We're all very pleased our dear friend was able to join us. That will be all."

"I'm so sorry, my lord," the red-faced usher spluttered. "He looked… I thought—"

"It's forgotten. Go." Lord Carlisle dismissed the usher, then turned to Jane. His voice lowered. "Do you mind moving down a seat so Xavier can sit next to me?"

Captain Grey frowned. "Unnecessary. I've already interrupted enough."

"No, I don't mind." Jane scrambled out of the way and waved a hand toward her vacated seat. "Please. Sit next to your friend."

He inclined his head and took his seat.

The lighting was too dim to make out the crystalline blue of his eyes or the long black lashes that framed them. But Jane didn't need lighting to recall every angle of his chiseled features or the careless tumble of wavy black hair against the stark white of his cravat. Every inch of him was seared into her memory.

Well, every properly (but disappointingly) clothed inch, that was. Nothing could hide the strong thighs encased in buckskin breeches or the thickly muscled arms filling out the sleeves of his expertly tailored jacket.

Heaven help her. She was going to be a hairsbreadth away from this gorgeous man for the next three hours. She absolutely, positively, couldn't swoon. Or throw herself into his arms. His thick, powerful arms.

Her breath caught. This was impossible. He'd been seated next to her for less than five seconds and already her heart thundered as though she were running for her life. Perhaps she *should* be. Captain Grey wasn't good for one's reputation… or one's heart.

Everyone knew that. He'd returned from war in a fugue state, and even before that, he hadn't been considered a catch. Not by Society. He wasn't rich. He wasn't heir to a coronet. And he'd always had the same air of danger and un-predictability that clung to him even now.

He appeared confident, graceful, and deadly. No wonder the usher had hesitated. Captain Grey moved more like a hunter than a gentleman. Those piercing blue eyes could freeze a duke right in his tracks.

Or a bluestocking spinster.

She lowered her lashes. There was no way she was going to be able to pay any attention to this opera. She was too aware of his intoxicating proximity, of the rise and fall of his chest, of the way his eyes... were looking right at her? Her leg started bouncing with nerves. He'd caught her *staring*. She slid a little lower in her chair.

Whatever color she'd flushed before was no-where near the crimson she must be blushing now.

He hunched closer so that his shoulder was touching hers. "Any idea what they're warbling about on stage?"

Oh, lord. She had no idea how her heart wasn't exploding right out of her chest. His *shoulder*. Was touching *hers*. On *purpose*.

"Er..." Her mind went blank. Captain Grey was actually talking to her. And expecting a re-ply. *Think*. What opera was this? She forced her gaze to the dueling sopranos. "That's... Ismene and Antigona. They're vexed that Creon won't bury Polynices because he started a war."

His eyes widened. "You speak Italian?"

She shook her head. "Greek. *Antigone* was a play before it was an opera. I must've read it a hundred times."

He blinked.

She let her words trail off. *Stop. Talking.* One must not admit to reading ancient Greek plays hundreds of times. Bluestockings do not leave a coquettish impression. One must strive to be enchanting and irresistible.

Her well-read mind failed to summon any actionable ideas.

His lips quirked. "I haven't read a book in years, so I suppose I ought to pay attention while the plot is being dramatized right in front of me." He turned his gaze back to the stage.

There. Jane tried not to crawl under her seat and die. This was what happened when she showed her excessive love for reading. Nothing. Nothing at all happened. That was exactly why she was so forgettable.

Yet she could think of nothing compelling to say or alluring to do. She couldn't believe she'd already lost his attention after having had it for such a brief moment. She was so… *Jane.*

Would it have been better to say she'd only read *Antigone* once? Or to claim she had no idea why those people were dancing about the stage with swords and lots of sobbing? Perhaps the wisest course would've been to—

His shoulder. She stopped breathing. His shoulder was still touching hers. He had

remained hunched down as if, any minute now,
they might once again be whispering like bosom
friends.

She shivered. If only!

It wasn't just that he was the most exquisitely
attractive man she'd ever laid eyes upon. He was
a soldier and a hero. An officer. Military men
were loyal, and heroic and strong and delicious.

Do not overthink, she admonished herself.
Proximity meant nothing. It was just a play. Just
a shoulder. He wasn't going to whisk her into the
shadows for a carnal interlude (not that she would
have objected) and he certainly wasn't in any
danger of losing his mind and proposing marriage. He planned on disappearing from Society
altogether.

But first, she was going to have to spend an
evening shoulder-to-shoulder with the one person she would *never* be able to get out of her
mind.

Chapter Three

AT HALF NINE the next morning, Jane tilted a wingback chair beneath the locked door to her private library. Such measures were unlikely to keep Isaac out if her brother were truly determined to enter, but the barred door would at least prevent Egui the devil-cat from leaping onto her head whilst she searched for guidance among her books.

Provided the cat wasn't in here already, lying in wait.

She peered about the library suspiciously but saw no sign of the potbellied gray demon.

Not that one ever did, until it was too late.

With a last look over her shoulder, she began to walk along the rows of books in search of inspiration. Something in one of these tomes was bound to help her get noticed. Perhaps no strategy could win her a suitor, but if she could be *desirable*, for once in her life...

She ran a finger along the spines and sighed. The novels were no use. They were full of perfect, beautiful maidens whose greatest challenge was deciding which rich, devoted beau she should take for a husband.

Jane was in no such predicament. Just the night before, she'd had her first conversation with an eligible bachelor in weeks and made a pretty botch of it by babbling about her obsession with ancient tragedies.

Her life wasn't a tragedy, at least. Other people were forced to the altar. She had narrowly escaped that fate and would just have to die an old maid. Was that not a blessing? A bad marriage had no advantage over spinsterhood.

To gain a husband, she would have to relinquish the freedoms she currently took for granted. Isaac often traveled for weeks at a time, which did leave her lonely, but who was to say a husband would not do the same?

Her brother loved her, which made for far more comfortable interactions than the silent, frigid meals shared by bitter couples that only wed for money or titles or because their parents had betrothed them while still in the womb, or other such nonsense.

She wasn't rich enough to attract fortune hunters on the strength of her dowry alone, but Isaac provided her with any pin money she requested without question. She could solicit the gowns she desired, attend any routs she wished, purchase any manuscripts she—

Ah. There.

She'd hidden the little book of erotic sketches inside the hollowed-out pages of a treatise on the evolution of various embroidery stitches across the centuries. She doubted Isaac would take it upon himself to research such a topic—and, besides, he had his own library—but one could never be too cautious. If she were to ruin her disappointingly pristine reputation, she wished to do so by *enjoying* illicit pleasures, not just by reading about them.

Or staring openmouthed.

Each illustration depicted a man and a woman in positions she could scarcely fathom. She'd perused these pages dozens of times, and still a few of them seemed impossible no matter which way she turned the book.

She sighed. Sketches couldn't convey the feel and scent and taste of lovemaking. To truly understand, she would have to experience the wonder for herself.

Which, in her position, would be an extremely unlikely occurrence.

From a certain perspective, it was almost too bad that she had been born into gentility. She wouldn't wish to trade her position in society for life in the rookeries, but there *was* an elegant middle tier: demimondaines.

Some of those women were wealthier and more sophisticated than the highest echelons of the *haut ton* and could select their lovers at will.

Rumors of carnal liaisons enhanced, rather than ruined, their reputations.

The only individuals enjoying somewhat comparable freedoms in Polite Society were the rakes—and even then, their debauchery could only go so far.

Respectable women, on the other hand, had no such privilege. The only way for a female to take a lover without ruining her name in the process was to marry... or to be so clandestine that no one was ever the wiser.

Realistically, only one of those options was open to Jane—and it wasn't marriage. The eligible men of her acquaintance had had four-and-twenty years to ask for her hand, and couldn't be bothered to ask her to dance.

Much less to perform acts of... whatever it was the inked couple was doing in this particular sketch. She turned the illustration around. It still looked like the same position. She wasn't certain it was erotic, but it was certainly *interesting*.

And tempting. While she wouldn't trade the freedoms of spinsterhood for a cold, loveless marriage, she would happily trade her lonely, monotonous days for nights of heated passion.

With the right man.

The image of Captain Grey's handsome visage rose to mind. As it did two hundred times a day. Would *she* have a clandestine affair with Captain Grey? Absolutely. The question was, would *he?*

Not when she lacked the basic ability to attract a man's interest.

She sighed. The thing about marriage was that one was rather required to have intimate encounters with one's spouse if one intended to beget heirs. The thing about secret affairs was that lovemaking was about pleasure, not practicality, and one only participated in carnal relations with those they desired.

And Jane was plainly undesirable.

She might have said invisible, were it not for that brief, whispered conversation and the subtle press of his shoulder against hers. She clutched the book to her chest. He had *seen* her. And spoken to her. And treated her like a friend, if only a temporary one.

None of which meant he'd be eager to lie with her but, oh, would such a liaison not be *perfect?*

Her shoulders fell. If it weren't completely out of the question, of course. At this hour, he was doubtlessly en route to his cottage in Chelmsford, and she was stuck here in this town house with her brother for the rest of the Season. For the rest of her life.

Even *if* she had managed to besot the captain with nothing more than the brush of her shoulder and a love of Greek playwrights, 'twould all be for naught. By the time she saw him again—if that day ever came—he would have long since found someone else. Someone memorable.

"Jane?" A loud knock thundered against the door.

Her brother. With shaking fingers, she fumbled the little book back inside the tome on decorative sewing and shoved it back in place amongst all the other volumes.

The door rattled against the chair propped beneath its handle. "I say, Jane. Are you blocking the entrance to your *library?*"

She dashed over to the door and lugged the heavy wingback chair back toward the fireplace. Panting, she shoved a damp tendril of hair off her forehead and flung open the library door.

"Don't be absurd, Isaac. Why on earth would I block the entrance to—*yeeaaaghh!*"

Egui the Satan-cat leapt from her brother's arms to the front of her bodice, his razor-sharp claws scraping all the way through her shift as he slid gleefully to the floor and shot off into the shadows.

"I wish you wouldn't tease him so," Isaac admonished her. "He never gets out of sorts unless he's around you."

She smiled through gritted teeth. "I shall endeavor to pay him less attention. Did you need something?"

"I'm afraid so. I've been called away to a meeting with the board of future fish farmers down in Exeter, and I have to leave in the next few minutes if I'm to miss the snowstorm heading this way. Can you ensure Egui is comfortable

while I'm away? It should only be a couple of
weeks at the most, but one never knows when it
comes to men and their herrings."

"Yes, yes, lovely," Jane answered automati-
cally, her heart pounding.

This was her opportunity to make her own
fate! With her brother away, no one would know
whether spinster Jane Downing was home alone
with her books or had slipped off for the night.
She could be in Chelmsford by luncheon.

If it didn't occur to Captain Grey to seduce
her, well, she would just have to seduce him. And
if he was not at home—or, worse, rejected her
outright—there were plenty of inns in Essex, and
she'd be back in London this time tomorrow
morning with nobody the wiser.

But first, she needed Isaac to depart as
quickly as possible so that she could hurry on her
way. "You go ahead, brother dear. Egui will be a
delight. Enjoy your meeting without a further
worry."

"You're marvelous, Jane, truly. I don't know
what I would do without you." He kissed both of
her cheeks, patted her arm, and then sank to his
knees to bid farewell to his demon spawn.
"Egui... Egui... C'mere, puss. Come say goodbye
to Papa."

Jane made no attempt to hide the roll of her
eyes at the singsong baby voice her manly elder
brother affected when he spoke to his cat. Nor did
she attempt to hide her fury and disbelief when

the potbellied fur-monster strolled out from between the bookcases with his head up and his sil-
ver tail high, docile as you please.

Egui leapt into Isaac's open arms with nary a
claw in sight. He stretched his spine, purring
loudly. As Isaac cradled his beloved pet to his
chest, Egui lifted his languid gaze over his master's shoulder and made direct eye contact with
Jane.

She could swear the little beast smirked.

Isaac rose to his feet and brushed gray hairs
from his breeches. "Thanks again, Jane. I owe
you enormously. Be good, kitten. I'll see you
both in a fortnight."

She smiled. Egui slipped beneath the hem of
her gown and began to shred her stockings.

Teeth gritted, Jane all but shoved Isaac out
the door. "No problem, brother. Anytime. Have a
good trip. Don't bring back any fish larvae. I love
you."

"Love you too, Jane. You're one in a mil-
lion." With a last buss to her cheek, Isaac was
down the hall and gone.

As soon as she heard the front door close,
Jane bent over and yanked Egui from her bleeding ankle—then immediately dropped him when
he let out an ear-piercing caterwaul. The last
thing she needed was for Isaac to run back and
spend the next two hours lecturing her on his an-
gelic pet's misunderstood intentions.

Before Egui could test his claws on her other ankle, she hurried out of the library and raced upstairs to her bedchamber. Her lady's maid stood before the open wardrobe with a pile of freshly laundered linens in her arms.

"Martha! Splendid timing. Help me put together a valise with... a week's worth of clothing." That was shamelessly optimistic, but Jane supposed it was better to have clean clothes and not need them than it was to attempt a seduction whilst swathed in week-old garments. "Perhaps a small trunk."

"At once, Miss Downing." Martha placed the linens on a shelf and went to fetch a traveling trunk. "Where are we going?"

"To..." Jane swallowed. If the whole purpose of this desperate endeavor was to embark on a brief, clandestine affair, the last person who should bear witness was a servant under Isaac's employ. She would have to go alone. "You shall have a week's holiday, effective immediately. I am visiting a sick friend, and it should be better for all of us if you don't fall ill yourself."

Martha's eyes sparkled. Jane had a strong suspicion the girl was sweet on one of the footmen and would not in the least begrudge a few days away from her mistress. Inter-staff liaisons were strongly discouraged, of course, but given that Jane was off to seduce a man who didn't know her from Princess Charlotte, she could hardly stand in the way of others' passion.

She began to pile shifts and stockings into the small trunk. "One tiny request, Martha. Can you please mind Egui for me while I'm gone?"

Martha blanched and shook her head wildly. "Oh, ma'am, please don't make me! I'd druther play nurse to lepers than spend one second alone with that cat. I don't think he... cares for me much."

Of course not. Jane's temples began to pound. Egui hated everyone except Isaac. Perhaps 'twas better to put one of the male servants in charge. "Very well. Go have Dunbar summon a hack. And send up a footman to carry down this trunk. I wish to leave at once."

Martha bobbed and nodded and dashed out of the bedchamber before her mistress could change her mind.

Jane had already pushed Egui from her thoughts. At least for the moment. The more pressing disaster was what clothes she might don to instill lust in a man's breast.

She scowled as she combed through her uninspiring wardrobe. How was she meant to seduce a dashing military captain when she'd failed to attract the attention of any other gentlemen of her acquaintance? She stuffed her embroidery kit next to the gowns. Perhaps she could lower a few bodices during the ride to Essex.

Jane was just latching the trunk when Martha returned with a pair of footmen, who immediately hefted it and awaited further instruction.

Martha wrung her hands. "Your hack is waiting, ma'am. Are you sure I oughtn't accompany you?"

"No, thank you. You've earned your holiday. Clive, Malcolm, I'll need you to mind Egui for me while I'm—"

Both footmen dropped the trunk and stared at her in horror. "You *cannot* mean it! I— We— *That cat*—"

Jane raised her eyes heavenward and let out a loud, long-suffering sigh. No intelligent person *wished* to mind Egui, but she was only the one foolish enough to have promised. He would now be her sole responsibility until Isaac's return, romantic encounter or not. "Let me be clear. I am going to be inside that hack and on my way within the next five minutes. If Egui is in a sealed basket upon my lap, he goes with me. If he is not—"

Clive and Malcolm fled the room without a backward glance.

Martha stared at the empty doorway, the forgotten trunk, and then her mistress. "Er... shall I summon the butler, perhaps?"

Jane shook her head. "By now, everyone is searching for that odious cat. Come on, then. You take that side, and I'll take this one."

With only minor damage to the wainscoting, she and Martha managed to get the trunk down the stairs and over to the front door, where the horrified butler and hack driver rushed forward

to relieve them of their unseemly burden and es-
cort Jane to the coach.

No sooner had her derrière touched the worn
squab of the hack than Clive and Malcolm raced
from the town house with a rocking, screeching
wicker basket held aloft between them and only
mild scratch marks upon their triumphant faces.

She held out her arms for the basket.

Egui, it seemed, was destined to play chaperone on her quest for a romantic encounter. Marvelous. She might not meet with success, but the
adventure could hardly fail to be a memorable
one.

Chapter Four

DESPITE THE ICY WIND and blinding snow, perspiration clung to Captain Xavier Grey's brow as he crashed an axe onto one of the few retrievable tree trunks still visible in the white blanket behind his small cottage.

When he'd sent his handful of servants up to Chelmsford a fortnight ago to prepare his domicile, the climate had been cold, but clear. When he'd sent his staff on holiday for the remainder of that fortnight while he visited friends in London, Xavier had actually looked forward to returning to his cottage a day or two before his servants. The solitude would do him good.

The storm, less so.

Provisions would last a week, two at the most. Perhaps that was plenty. Perhaps it was not. Keeping warm would be critical. He swung the axe one last time and then began hauling the logs indoors.

No one had predicted a snowstorm. He supposed that was the very nature of... well, *nature*. Unpredictability. What had begun as a lovely snowfall now threatened to entomb them all in their homes. He added the last of the logs to the reserve pile.

A chill rippled across his skin as he barred the front door against the bone-cold wind. 'Twas ironic. He had hoped never to be trapped any-where again, and now here he was, doing it to himself. The fact that it was voluntary this time — all openings were sealed to keep out the snow, not to keep in the man — ought to have eased his rising panic.

It didn't.

He began to stalk the corridors of his old, fa-miliar cottage. The kitchen was clean and cold. The dining room: dark. The library: silent. The servants' quarters: vacant. The master bedroom: lonesome. The entire cottage was devoid of com-pany or stimulation. Just a restless ex-captain, alone with his thoughts... and his memories.

Xavier wasn't fond of either companion.

He might have left the battlefield, but his mind was still at war. He could never erase the horrors he'd seen. Nor the role he'd played.

His skin crawled. He had learned things about himself that he would do anything to for-get. He'd set off in search of honor, of heroism. Instead, he'd found evil. All around, and inside himself.

And he'd been *rewarded* for it.

It was bitter irony that he'd returned home without a scratch on him when more honorable men—*better* men—had returned in pieces, or not at all. His childhood friend Bartholomew Blackpool was in want of a leg... and the man's twin brother had died defending their country.

Xavier would never tell Bart how fortunate Edmund was that a bullet had pierced him before the French soldiers found him.

There were far worse fates than death. Xavier would know.

He shrugged out of his coat and shirtsleeves and washed up at a basin filled with water.

It was no use. He would never feel clean. Nor should he.

He sighed. It was just as well that he was stuck out here without any servants. He didn't deserve company, and he certainly didn't deserve being waited on. He hoped his staff was wise enough to wait out the inclement weather rather than attempt to reach the cottage during a snowstorm. The roads would quickly become a death trap.

He pulled on a fresh shirt and shoved his arms into his thickest coat. Dressing warmly would allow him to better ration the firewood.

The parlor was the only chamber with a small blaze in its hearth. He stirred the embers with a poker. Night would fall in a few hours, and he didn't want the fire to die in the meantime.

A knock sounded upon his front door.

Frowning, Xavier replaced the poker and strode to the entryway. Aside from Lord Carlisle and a few local Chelmsford residents, nobody knew Xavier had resumed residence in his little cottage. Who on Earth would be knocking at his door? Better yet, why? He swung open the door.

He nearly choked in surprise. "*Miss Downing?* What the devil are you doing here? Has something happened?"

Her eyes rounded. "You remember me?"

"I'm not *senile*. We were introduced years ago, and we sat beside each other last night." He scanned her for possible injuries. "Are you all right? Was there a carriage accident?"

She shook her head. "Nothing like that. I… was in the neighborhood. Not far at all. So I thought I'd pay a visit."

"On *foot?*" He shook his head to clear it of disbelief.

The daft woman stood upon his stoop with a battered trunk and a shrieking picnic basket. From the snaking rectangular trail in her wake, she'd lugged her trunk behind her from somewhere down the road. By herself. In a snowstorm. With a hissing basket.

He snatched the possessed basket from her hand and hauled her inside the house. It was frightful outside. He swung the trunk inside the entryway and slammed the door tight against the cold and wind. Already snowflakes covered the floor. The warmth of the fire was just a memory.

He grabbed her by the shoulders and forced himself not to shake some sense into her. "You cannot possibly have believed this to be appropriate conditions for a stroll down country roads. Are you *mad?*"

"Just... a bit chilled, I think..." she said through chattering teeth.

He dragged her into the parlor and placed her in the chair closest to the fire. "I'm going to start a pot of tea, and once you've drunk every drop of it, I expect a full accounting of what brings you to my doorstep with a trunk and a—"

The basket shrieked and hurled itself against the closest wall.

"—and a *cat.*" He narrowed his eyes at her. "Do. Not. Move."

Her huge brown eyes blinked up at him. "Why are *you* starting the tea? Haven't you a cook or a butler or—"

"I'm afraid uninvited guests don't always have the luxury of arriving when the staff isn't away on holiday."

Her expression brightened, but she made no further move to stop him from fetching tea. Confounding woman. He stalked to the kitchen.

Hellfire. Three years at war had taught him more than he ever wished to know about being self-sufficient. But the last thing he was equipped to handle was a bluestocking spinster with long chestnut curls, sparkling brown eyes, and a rabid cat. A creature that, from the sound of it, had finally managed to escape its basket and streak down the hall toward Xavier's library.

Bluestocking, he reminded himself. Of course her ball of fur felt more at home in a library. Besides, the cat was not the problem. His problem was the innocent, unmarried, unaccompanied maiden seated in the parlor of an infamous, immoral, cynical ex-soldier.

Wonderful. He had sworn to never again cause harm to another human, yet he'd destroyed Miss Downing's reputation merely by allowing her through his door.

Then again, perhaps the situation was not so dire. There were no witnesses to her utter lack of judgment. If he could pack her off to—wherever she'd come from—before his servants arrived, they might both be able to pretend this misadventure had never happened.

In fact, that was likely the reason her eyes had lit up when she'd learned there were no servants. The poor thing was finally concerned about the state of her reputation.

A shrill whistle filled the air as the water reached a boil. He turned to pick up the small towel he used for handling hot objects and stilled.

The towel was now ribbons. And flecked with short gray hairs.

He frowned. He could've sworn the cat had taken off for the library. He'd heard its claws clicking across the wooden floor. Was he to believe that had been a *feint?* That the cat had purposefully made excess noise to throw him off the trail, and then returned on silent paws while

Xavier's back was turned in order to shred a perfectly good tea towel? Ridiculous.

Yet the yellow square of cloth was now rubbish.

"I believe the water's boiling," Miss Downing called from the parlor. "The whistle means—"

"I know what the whistle means." He glanced around. Where the devil were the rest of the towels? He yanked off his ascot and used it to lift the shrieking kettle from the stove. He placed it on a tray with milk, honey, and two tea settings, and carried it into the parlor.

She blinked at him in confusion. "Did you lose your cravat in the kitchen?"

He set down the tray on the tea table between the two chairs. "You know who gets to ask questions? *I* get to ask questions. Drink your tea."

"I just—"

"Drink." Fingers trembling, he poured each of them a serving of tea. He didn't *wish* to ask questions. But here she was. What was he supposed to do? He lifted his cup to his lips as he considered his next steps.

Her nose wrinkled. "You drink yours without milk or honey?"

He slanted her a dark look.

"Right." She lowered her lashes and reached for the milk. "You ask the questions."

Not anymore. Old dread crept over his skin. He wasn't certain he could question anyone ever again. He was done with interrogations, with extracting answers from unwilling captives.

While Miss Downing had descended upon him of her own free will, the snow and moonless night would keep them both prisoner until dawn. He would not treat her like one.

"So," he said instead. "You have a cat. Does it have a name?"

"Egui," she mumbled against her teacup.

Egui? He frowned. Odd name for a cat, but who was he to judge? He wasn't stable enough for a pet.

"Does Egui always enjoy ripping cloth to shreds?"

She lowered her teacup in horror. "He ate your *cravat?*"

"No, of course n—" Or had he? Xavier gritted his teeth. He'd placed his wadded-up cravat on the counter next to the shredded towel when he'd brought the tea tray into the parlor. What were the odds it was still where he'd left it? "One moment."

He rose on stiff legs and marched into the kitchen. His jaw clenched when he caught sight of his cravat. Wonderful.

Egui, two points. Xavier, none. His cravat now resembled a linen octopus. With a discarded hairball instead of eyes.

He returned to the parlor and dropped heavily back into his chair. "Yes. Egui ate my cravat."

She winced. "He eats... everything. He's a very peckish cat. His other favorite pastime is hide-and-seek. I recommend locking your bed-chamber if you intend to sleep."

"Delightful," he murmured. "And to think they claim *dogs* are a man's best friend."

She took a dainty sip of tea. "He's more like... family. I'm afraid I'm stuck with him."

And now Xavier was too, because his un-planned houseguest thought of the beast as fam-ily. Ravenous, demented family.

This couldn't continue for long. He needed a plan.

He also had a thousand questions, but no wish to interrogate her. Perhaps he wouldn't have to. A young lady like Miss Downing was unlikely to have ulterior motives. Although he was hard-pressed to come up with a rational explanation for her presence, and under such unlikely circum-stances.

"I couldn't help but notice you brought lug-gage," he said presently. "But no chaperone. Or carriage."

She flashed a nervous smile over the rim of her teacup. "It's the funniest thing. You're right that I have no chaperone, but I did rent a hack. The driver refused to take the horses any further than the Dog & Whistle due to the ice and snow. For the same reason, the innkeeper was com-pletely without rooms to let. My driver accepted a pallet in the mews, which of course wouldn't do for a young lady. So I walked here. But don't worry. It was less than a quarter mile."

Something was funny, all right. Xavier tapped his fingers together. "I'm so glad there's a reasonable, not-remotely-questionable explanation for dragging a cat and a trunk through a snowstorm to a bachelor's private cottage. Your brother will love to hear this."

She jumped. "You know Isaac?"

He stared at her. "Why do you think me incapable of remembering people?"

She cleared her throat. "I would prefer you didn't mention this visit to him, that's all."

"I would prefer not mentioning it to anyone. Come morning, the snow will melt enough to return you to the Dog & Whistle and commission a driver willing to take you right back home to London."

Her shoulders relaxed. "I can stay the night? Here?"

He held up his palms. "Did you expect me to offer the mews?"

She beamed at him. "I knew you wouldn't. You're too steadfast and honorable."

"I'm too *what?* I'm nothing of the sort!"

"Of course you are. You're a soldier and a hero. Anyone would be safe in your company."

"You've no idea what being a good soldier means. I'm a bringer of death and destruction. And the worst person of my acquaintance. You shouldn't be anywhere near me."

She shook her head. "That was during the war, whilst defending innocent civilians from Napoleon's tyranny. The very definition of heroic."

He raked a hand through his hair. If only he *were* the kind of man she painted him to be. "The point is, you shouldn't be here. You're a well-bred young lady with a fine reputation, and if we are quite lucky, you might be able to keep it that way."

She held his gaze. "Part of that is true."

He almost laughed. Miss Downing was the very embodiment of innocence and purity. "I'm afraid I don't follow. Are you claiming you're *not* a chaste young lady in possession of a pristine reputation?"

"Of course I am. But I don't wish to be." She set down her teacup and bit her lip. "Might I be your mistress?"

Chapter Five

XAVIER LEAPT FROM HIS CHAIR in horror. "Absolutely not!"

Miss Downing's rosy lower lip trembled. "Is it because I'm plump?"

"Is it—" He rubbed a hand over his face. "Your body is not the problem. Your virginity is the problem."

She nodded. "Precisely!"

He gripped the side of his chair. "Have you completely lost your mind?"

Her gaze was direct. "I spent the four-hour carriage ride obsessing over every angle, in fact, and I'm convinced the advantages far outweigh any drawbacks." She fumbled for her reticule. "In fact, I made a chart—"

"No charts." Xavier waved away the folded scrap of parchment. His world was slipping off its axis. He was definitely going to need to sit back down.

But not too close to Miss Downing. He dragged his chair a few inches farther away before sinking into it. "Do enlighten me."

She leaned forward to pat the edge of his armrest. "At ease, Captain Grey. I'm proposing a temporary union for carnal purposes, not a visit to the altar."

"I'm ever so relieved," he drawled. Their predicament had only got worse. "Pray continue."

"Simply put, I would like to experience passion. Preferably with you." Her cheeks flushed, but she kept his gaze. "And since you're not in Town for the Season, I imagine there are fewer opportunities for dalliances, and—" Her breath caught. "You haven't got a mistress already, have you?"

"I find myself between lovers at the moment." Or from now on. He certainly wasn't going to begin with her.

She sagged against the back of her chair. "Thank heavens. I don't see how I could have survived the humiliation, had you already possessed a mistress."

"Mm." He nodded. "We are fortunate indeed to have avoided all awkwardness."

Her eyes narrowed. "Are you employing sarcasm with me?"

His fingers tightened on his breeches. "What else am I to employ? I certainly shan't employ my *member*. Of course you cannot be my mistress! I hardly make it a practice to debauch virgins, and what's more—"

"But that's what makes it perfect." She leaned forward earnestly. "I could have attempted to talk any number of rakes or roués into an alliance, but I don't wish to lie with someone who has already lain with twenty others. Nor would I like my first experience to be with someone whose face or touch repulses me. I simply wish to be *wanted*, by someone I also want, and enjoy a night or two of mutual pleasure."

He stared at her over his steepled fingers and tried to think how best to proceed. Without ruining them both. He found everything about her—from her soft curves to her bookishness to her startling frankness—undeniably attractive, but that didn't stop this proposal from being the worst idea he'd heard in years.

Miss Downing plainly failed to comprehend the irrevocability of what she was offering. What she was suggesting he become party to. She was an innocent in every sense. Her peers would not overlook such a transgression. She'd spent her life surrounded by books, not people. She might think that made her worldly, but it did not. The real world was a harsh place—an unfortunate reality she had yet to face, and with luck would never have to.

Presuming she didn't follow through on this plan. Or proposition other men when she failed to seduce Xavier. His muscles tightened.

While she might think she had devised the perfect, mutually pleasurable, secret arrangement, she did not know him well enough to know whether he had slept with every whore on the

Continent or whether he could be trusted to keep her debauched state a secret. She hadn't even asked.

He rubbed the back of his neck. Nothing was ever as simple as it sounded, especially when trying to predict other people. The *bon ton*, for example. The things people said did not necessarily correlate with the things they felt. And the behavior one witnessed in another person did not necessarily represent what they did when no one else was around.

The fact that she was willing to put her reputation in the palm of his hands based on nothing more substantial than consecutive seats at an opera *proved* her naïvety—and the need to keep her innocence intact.

If she was hell-bent on ruin, he would simply have to talk her out of it.

"Miss Downing," he began, keeping his voice as calm and rational as possible. "You are currently an innocent. Despite your or my personal feelings on the matter, young ladies such as yourself must remain virgins if they wish to continue being welcome members of Polite Society."

Her chin thrust forward. "I never claimed I wished to be part of Polite Society. If I am now, 'tis only on the fringes. *Wallflowers* are more popular than me. Apart from my brother, the only individuals who can even recall my name are the three who joined us at the theatre last night." She waved a hand. "Who, precisely, am I saving my maidenhead for?"

He blinked. "Your future husband?"

"What future husband?" Her eyes flicked skyward. "I'm not a particularly sought-after commodity on the Marriage Mart. I'm plump. I lack an impressive dowry. I'm well above the age most men find appealing. If I wish to experience passion, the only way of achieving that goal is by going after it myself."

If she was plump, it was in all the right areas. However, admitting his attraction to her would only convince her that this plan was the correct path. She was looking in the wrong place. He was not the man for her.

"The right person won't care about your age or your dowry, and you're just as pretty as your peers. If you throw away your maidenhead—on me or any bloke—you will *never* find a husband." He leaned back and crossed his arms. "I refuse to help you ruin your future."

Her fists clenched briefly. "Whatever assets I might bring to a marriage, my innocence is the least valuable. Try to be logical. The groom takes his bride's maidenhead in the first seconds, and then it's gone. So why bother at all? Besides, how would he even know, if I never tell him?"

He arched a brow. "You would lie?"

"I will never be in that situation in the first place." She pressed her lips into a white slash. "Most of the *beau monde* select their spouses

because the union is advantageous to their pock-
etbook or social status. I'm not only at peace with
mine—as a bluestocking and a spinster, I enjoy
more freedoms than most—I would not give
them up for a husband I didn't love." Her lips
curved. "Fortuitously, I wouldn't have to relinquish either for a mere lover."

"Just your maidenhead."

"By definition," she pointed out dryly. "Is
lovemaking not the *point* of taking a lover?"

Of course. But it didn't signify.

The risk of jeopardizing her chances of at-
tracting a future husband might not give her
pause, but her idealistic views didn't matter. He
drummed his fingers. *He* would not be a willing
party to her complete ruin. She should be on the
arm of some venerable duke or earl, not offering
her charms to a cynical ex-soldier. She was smart
and beautiful. He didn't deserve her esteem and
he certainly didn't deserve her virginity.

His chest tightened as he thought of all the
ways it could go wrong. She was innocent. He
was a monster. Any relationship with him could
not end well. He had seen the darkest parts of the
world. He had *been* the darkest part of the world.
The shadows were where he belonged. Not with
her.

Not even for one night.

"I'm not against marriage," she said, her eyes
wide and vulnerable. "Or husbands. I simply
don't have the option. And after all this time, I've

come to appreciate what I *do* have. A brother who loves me. Enough books and pin money to keep me clothed and entertained. The freedom to do as I please. If I marry, my time, money, and freedoms will depend wholly on the whim of my husband. I don't think that's a very good trade." She held up a hand when he started to interrupt. "I could be wrong, I admit. That's why I'm here."

His eyebrows shot up. He was meant to be an experiment?

She clasped her hands together and leaned forward. "How do I know if the marriage bed is worth relinquishing the freedoms of spinsterhood? I cannot make an informed decision until I've experienced it for myself. If I dislike it, I'll simply never do it again. With marriage, I wouldn't have that luxury."

"That's your argument?" he said with a choked laugh. "You want me to have my wicked way with you just to find out if it's awful?"

"Not at all. I want to experience passionate, carnal relations with someone I can't resist. Someone strong." Her eyes met his without flinching. "Someone honorable. Someone I crave." Her low voice raked his soul. "And that man is you."

His breeches tightened in response to her words. Bloody hell. His entire body thrummed with awareness. This woman was intoxicating. Her cheeks were pale, her lips flushed, but her sensual brown eyes gazed right into his soul.

Of course he wanted her. He would have to be made of stone not to want her. And after a speech like that, he had to summon every ounce of his willpower to stay in his chair rather than carry her to bed and give her exactly what she'd asked for. Slowly. Deliciously. His body ached to make her his.

But he was not who she thought he was. Nor could he be.

"You say you desire an honorable man. That you believe *me* to be honorable. But anyone who accepts the gift of your body without a care for your heart or your future is deplorable, not honorable." This had gone on long enough. He rose from his chair. "I've secluded myself out here in this cottage to protect others from me, not to ruin them in my own home."

She leaped to her feet in response. "You don't want any woman, or you don't want me? If I were a light-skirt, we would already be naked. Or is there nothing about me that attracts you, and I've been wasting my breath since I got here?"

He grasped her shoulders and let his harsh voice betray his passion. "*Everything* about you attracts me. You think you're the only one with carnal dreams? There's not a man alive who wouldn't love to be in my shoes right now. To be this close to tasting your lips. To cover your body with mine."

Her nostrils flared. "There isn't a man in London who even knows my name."

He stepped back and shoved his thumbs into his waistband. "They know your name. They also know your brother would thrash them within an inch of their lives if they so much as touched you."

A choked laugh gurgled in her throat. *"Isaac?"*

The shock on her face indicated she'd never considered there might be any other explanation beyond her "plump" frame and modest dowry.

Xavier leaned closer. "You have no idea how tempting your offer is. Just like you have no idea what you're truly giving me permission to do with your mouth and your body."

"Don't I?" She fished a small sketchbook from her reticule. "I'm not going to be shocked by the mechanics of lovemaking. Not when I've studied an illustrated guide. Page fourteen: Riding backward. Page twenty-seven: Oral stimulation. Page—"

His lungs froze. How in Hades had she come into possession of such a thing? He snatched the book from her hand and threw it against the wall. "Enough."

"It's never enough." She grabbed the lapels of his coat and lifted her face to his. Her body fit perfectly against him. "Show me what I'm missing."

He couldn't move. Dear Lord, he could not push her away.

"One night," she whispered. "I'm already here. What happens next is up to us." She touched her lips to the edge of his jaw. "Send me away in the morning, but first give me one night of passion."

Her voice was soft, her eyes shuttered. Her mouth right there for the taking. Her body...

He forced himself to step back while he still had the strength to do so.

"I shall not be your experiment, Miss Downing. If you throw away your future, it won't be on me."

Chapter Six

JANE PIVOTED AWAY from Captain Grey as heat flooded her face. He didn't want her. She couldn't ignore the nausea in her belly or the hole in her chest. She had made her case with every wile available to her. Logic, physicality... even pleading.

And she could not have been rejected more soundly.

Failure cut deep. She crossed to the far wall on stiff legs and bent to retrieve the fallen sketchbook. Its long guarded illustrations had robbed her of countless nights of sleep. Now she couldn't even bear to look at it. She shoved it back into her reticule with trembling fingers.

The depictions of pleasure therein would have to remain theoretical.

She laid her reticule on the mantel and quit the parlor without a word. Captain Grey did not stop her. Why would he? There was nothing left to discuss.

Egui's abandoned wicker basket lay at the end of the corridor. If she didn't get the cat back in his basket, he would wreak havoc on Captain Grey's home. She took a deep breath and slowly let it out. Corralling Egui was a task she was familiar with. Challenging. Perilous. But not impossible.

Who would've believed it easier to catch a demon cat than the interest of a lonely soldier?

She made her way to the end of the hall and looped her arm through the handle of the basket. With luck, Egui hadn't destroyed the rest of Captain Grey's cravats during the course of their disastrous conversation. The evening would be uncomfortable enough without also owing the man an entirely new wardrobe.

"I need to find the cat," she called over her shoulder. "May I hunt in any open rooms?"

"You may do as you please," he replied from only a few feet away.

She spun about.

He stood at the doorway to the parlor, watching her. His blue gaze was inscrutable.

After a heartbeat, he disappeared back into the parlor.

She straightened her spine and smiled grimly. She could *not* do as she pleased. Not here and not anywhere. She couldn't have the man she wanted. Couldn't find the devil cat she *didn't* want. She couldn't even hop into a hack and go back home.

Her motives might have been foolish, but her plan had been sound. *Too* sound. Blasted snowstorm. It had seemed so fortuitous at the time, and now... Just another cosmic mockery.

Her brother was two hundred miles away. The servants suspected nothing. She'd changed hacks every half hour to make certain no single person knew where she'd been or where she was going. The Dog & Whistle had indeed been over capacity, providing her with a legitimate need for close, safe lodging. The relentless snow ensured her welcome inside the cottage.

And now she couldn't leave.

She slipped off her half boots in order to tread through the cottage more quietly. Calling to the cat would only give him fair warning. Her only hope was to catch him unawares—before he did the same to her.

First, she tried the kitchen. This was where Egui had somehow destroyed Captain Grey's cravat... Ah. There it was. A disgusting clump of wet fur and shredded linen. Right next to a similar pile of what once had been a tea towel of some kind. Lovely. Her brother's cat was a never-ending joy.

She stood on her toes to inspect the top of every surface and dropped to her knees to check below each stick of furniture. No sign of Egui. She returned to the corridor and shut the kitchen door tight behind her.

The next open doorway led to what must be the servants' quarters. The beds were made perfectly and the fireplaces had not been lit. Jane hugged herself against the chill. The empty rooms were far too cold for her, but Egui was blessed with a layer of steel-gray fur. The temperature would suit him fine, and his dusky coat would be almost impossible to detect in the quickly waning light.

Jane checked above every wardrobe and beneath every bed, but could find no trace of the missing cat.

She rarely did until it was too late.

Much like her interaction with Captain Grey, she supposed. She hadn't been able to protect herself from being wounded because she hadn't anticipated the source of the blow. *Non*-action hurt just as much as action. Perhaps even more so.

Her shoulders slumped. The wounds from Egui's sharp little claws would clear up in a week or two. But Captain Grey's outright rejection would leave its mark forever.

She sealed the door to the servants' quarters and crossed the hall into the dining room. A tall mahogany sideboard lined the perimeter. An oblong table with eight wooden chairs stood in the center. No hiding places. No sign of Egui. Jaw set, she stalked into the next room—and abruptly stopped in the doorway.

A library. Small, but comfortable. A chaise longue and a wingback chair faced the unlit fireplace.

The bookcases were few, but contained a respectable number of titles. She couldn't help but peruse them. Politics… agriculture… classics… *Fanny Hill!* She snatched the volume from the shelf and held it to her chest.

An erotic novel! She had *longed* to read such a thing, but hadn't wanted to have to hide more than one book from her brother. There might not be explicit imagery within these pages, but anything calling itself *Memoirs of a Woman of Pleasure* was something she wouldn't wish to explain how it came to be in her possession some night over dinner.

Not that it was appropriate material here, either.

She slid the book back into its slot amongst the others. Reading about fictional erotic encounters while under the same roof as Captain Grey would only make her yearn for him all the more. 'Twas better for both of them to have her curiosity remain unsatisfied.

Although it was deliciously tempting to borrow it just for the night…

Forcing herself to abandon the book, she inspected above and within each shelf in search of the missing cat. Nothing. Not even a telltale gray hair to indicate he'd ever entered the room. She exited the library and shut the door firmly behind her. And swallowed hard.

The last remaining room was Captain Grey's bedchamber. She hesitated at the open doorway.

Flickering orange light emanated from the fireplace, giving the room a soft, warm glow. Directly across was a large four-poster bed with thick emerald curtains. An armoire stood to one side, and a table bearing a pitcher and basin stood on the other. Yet she couldn't take her eyes from the bed.

What might it have been like, to join him beneath the blankets? Hot, obviously. Thrilling. Unforgettable.

But she would never know.

She clenched her fingers against the unbidden twist in her stomach. The truth couldn't be plainer. Captain Grey wasn't just an ex-soldier. He was a war hero. A leader of men. If he wanted something, he took it.

Therefore, he didn't want *her*. If he did, she'd already be naked.

She set down the basket and knelt to peer beneath the bed. No cat. She tightened her jaw. Where in the world was he hiding?

A thump sounded in the doorway and she sprang to her feet in alarm.

Not Egui. Excitement infused her veins. *Captain Grey*. Delivering *her* trunk to *his* bedchamber.

Chapter Seven

XAVIER TOOK a healthy step back from Miss Downing's trunk. She was standing in his bedchamber. He should be far, far away. Not staring at her long, shimmering hair or imagining the feel of those voluptuous curves beneath his hands. Her untouched innocence attracted him just as viscerally as her beauty. He looked away. She was not for him.

He shoved his hands behind his back to shield them from her—and from temptation. He didn't need to glimpse the silken unmentionables she might have packed for a seduction. He didn't want to picture her alone in his bed, naked, and thinking of him.

Nor could he imagine how he was meant to make it through the long wintry night with his sanity—and her virginity—intact.

He kept his voice authoritative and firm. "My cottage has no guest quarters, so you'll have to sleep in the master chamber. I, of course, shall take the servants' quarters."

Miss Downing's rosy lips fell open and a flash of renewed hurt dulled her eyes. "You don't intend to share your bed with me?"

He rubbed his face. "Forgive me for pointing out that I didn't even intend to share my home with you.

If you have developed any illusions about me or my character, please do away with them posthaste. I live alone for a reason. As an innocent, you may not fully understand the ramifications of your proposal, but I am not fit to be a husband and I *shan't* be your despoiler."

Her chin rose. "I'm looking for a lover, not a husband. Do you think me too naïve to have foreseen a broken heart in my future? I saw that coming the moment I laid eyes on you." Her voice broke as she turned away. "I'd just hoped to share a few pleasurable moments first."

He frowned. She'd come here *expecting* to be cast aside post coitus and still felt it merited the experience? Zeus, was she innocent! Very well. He would have to be strong enough for them both.

To deflect her attention, he gestured at the bedside table. "There's fresh water in the pitcher, and the bed linens are freshly laundered. There's more than enough firewood to last the night. If you can think of anything else—"

"I think it's ridiculous for you not to sleep in your own bed."

He stared at her. "I can't very well sleep in my bed if you're in it, and I will *not* remand you to the servant's quarters."

"Why must either of us sleep somewhere else?" She crossed her arms. "Either I am already ruined—in which case, there's no reason for us not to share the best chamber—or else no one will learn that I was ever here. In which case, there's no reason for us not to share the best chamber."

His jaw clenched. "No."

Her brown eyes blazed. "*'No?'* Your argument against sound logic is simply *'No?'*"

Before he could cement her distaste at his autocratic nature by pointing out that it was his bed, his house, and his rules, a ten-pound clawed tornado leaped from above the four-poster canopy and latched itself to Xavier's head with an ear-splitting shriek.

He grunted and shook his head free of the cat—or tried to—but the creature dug in its claws and held on tight. He was wearing the damn thing like a bonnet. Gritting his teeth, he clapped his hands around its soft belly and thrust it from his head. Warmth trickled down one cheek. Xavier was certain he was also missing a fair chunk of hair, but perhaps it would work to his advantage.

No maiden would be overcome with arousal by a man who looked like he'd lost a battle with a lion.

He held the writhing, hissing creature toward her with stiff arms. "Your cat, madam."

Eyes filled with horror, she swung a thick basket up from the floor and trapped her pet inside. "I am incredibly sorry. I never meant for him to hurt you. He's... high-spirited, and unused to strangers or strange places, and I'm afraid he—"

"It's fine."

"It's not fine." Gaze soft, she lifted a hand toward his cheek. "You're bleeding."

He jerked away. "I survived three years at war. I won't be felled by a cat."

Presuming it wasn't rabid. From the racket it was making inside that basket, Xavier couldn't discount the possibility.

"You're just as ill-tempered as he is." Miss Downing clutched the howling basket to her chest and scowled. "If you won't let me tend your wound, will you direct me to my coat? If we're to avoid accidents of another kind, he needs a brief trip out-of-doors before we settle in for the night."

Xavier sighed. The last thing he needed was Egui piddling all over the cottage. And with the weather as it was, he certainly couldn't send Miss Downing out for even a moment. He reached for the basket. "Give it here."

She shook her head. "He truly distrusts strangers, and if anything were to happen to him, my—"

"Nothing's going to happen. Stay here where it's warm. Make yourself comfortable. The cat and I will return in a few moments."

Despite the emasculating lack of confidence in her expression, she at last relinquished the basket.

He inclined his head and quit the bedchamber.

Rather than go immediately outside, he headed for the servants' quarters. He might not be able to prevent the cat from attacking, but he'd be damned if he let it run away. Which left what?

The skinny, gray, potbellied devil-cat was unlikely to respect the sort of leash one might use with a dog. Xavier needed to fashion something as unusual as the cat itself. He twisted the cord from a bellpull into a figure eight and wrestled Egui's front paws into the holes as if it were a waistcoat. He looped the ends of the cord through the metal clasp of a leather belt and tied a solid knot.

There. A cat leash. He leaned back, satisfied. As long as he didn't let go of his end—and Egui refrained from attack—all would be well.

Xavier bundled the cat back into the basket and slipped on his coat and hat before slipping out into the blustery evening.

The icy wind robbed his lungs of air. Once his body adjusted to the frigid wind, he released Egui from his basket, careful to keep a firm hold on the safe end of the belt.

He couldn't contain a brief smile. Taking a demon cat for a piss in the snow couldn't be further from how he'd imagined spending his first night home, but Miss Downing and company were undeniably more entertaining. Even if he got a few new scars out of the escapade.

In fact, Egui might just be the key to saving them all. And not just because no man in his right mind would trust that cat anywhere near his bare arse.

Miss Downing, on the other hand... Xavier needed one hell of a plan to dissuade her from throwing away her virginity. A plan that stopped her from wanting *him*.

The easiest way would be to let her know exactly what sort of blackguard she was offering herself to, but his damnable pride hated the idea of resorting to such measures.

For one, tales of his misdeeds would rob her of a different sort of innocence. No one deserved that. And for two... she *liked* him. No matter how misplaced her faith in him might be, he hated to give it up. He just needed her to think of him as a friend, not a lover.

A friend who took her barmy cat for moonlit walks in the snow.

He turned his back to the wind and shivered. Yes, that was the answer. He would drown her in platonic politeness. Illustrate his relentless *friend*-ishness at every turn.

The best way to keep Miss Downing safe was to keep her at arm's length.

His fingers curled into fists. By devoting himself to the care and well-being of her cat and all other libido-killing topics, he would mold her impression of him until he squarely fit the role of friend and nothing more.

Xavier tucked the cat back into the basket and hurried into the cottage, away from the bitter cold. Once inside, he leaned against the door until sensation returned to his fingertips.

Lord, it was wretched outside. In the past few hours, the weather had only worsened.

He could build up the fire in the parlor, but firewood was limited. He'd told Miss Downing that there would be plenty to see her through the night, and that was true—but it meant extinguishing all the other fires in order to better ration the wood. If the blinding snowfall kept him from chopping more, he would need to preserve what they still had.

In the morning, he would shovel a path to the road and put Miss Downing on the first passing hack. Once she was on her way, he would take stock of his provisions and decide how to best fortify his cottage. And turn his life around. He shrugged out of his coat and knelt to release Egui from his basket.

At last free of its makeshift leash, the cat shot off down the corridor and out of sight.

Xavier pushed to his feet. He'd let Miss Downing know her pet had returned safely, and then he'd barricade himself in the servants' quarters until dawn.

This wasn't a mere challenge. This was his chance to prove he was no longer the monster he'd become.

He rolled his shoulders back. Just a handful of hours. Morning would be here before he knew it. He'd endured much worse fates than an unexpected visit by a voluptuous temptress.

He strode down the hall to his bedchamber, intending to knock softly lest Miss Downing be sound asleep.

The door was wide open. She was still there. Still clothed. And damnably seductive.

She sat on the sole stool, running a brush through her long, brown hair. The lustrous curls caught the light, entrancing him as they stretched and coiled about her. His heart quickened.

What would it be like to sink his fingers into that mass of soft, silken curls? To slide his hand behind her head as he brought her lips to his? Or to have a cascade of curls curtain him from both sides as she straddled his hips and leaned down to—

He rapped his fingers against the doorframe hard enough to draw blood. She glanced up, startled, and then smiled shyly. His heart skipped a beat.

Friend friend friend, he reminded himself, trying desperately to tear his gaze from hers. No looking, no touching, no lovemaking. His houseguest was one hundred percent out-of-bounds. But he kept his feet on the other side of the doorway to be safe.

"No problem with the cat." He cleared his throat when his voice came out raspier than expected. "Is there anything else you need before I turn in for the night?"

Her cheeks flushed a deep pink. "Would you mind terribly... helping me remove my gown?"

"Would I *what?*" he choked out, suddenly unable to breathe.

"It's just... Ladies' gowns are made with the expectation that one's maid will manage the lacing and unlacing." She gestured behind her. "I find myself incapable of the contortions necessary to unhook my gown and unbind my stays."

He swallowed hard and prayed for strength. "How did you plan to get dressed without a lady's maid?"

Her blush deepened. "I didn't plan to *be* dressed."

"Well done. Now I'm expected to play maid." He stalked forward to unlace her as quickly as possible.

"I did give you another option," she murmured. "I find the thought of both of us naked to be equally acceptable."

He groaned. It was going to be a long, hard night.

Literally.

Chapter Eight

XAVIER'S FIRST THOUGHT upon waking wasn't about the willing woman curled betwixt his bed linen... but only because he hadn't managed to sleep at all, for that very same reason.

Yes, the servants' quarters were uncomfortable in their strangeness. Without a fire in the hearth, his breath escaped his lungs in visible puffs of frigid air. But that was nothing. During the war, he'd slept in far less noble conditions. Beneath the rain, against the wind, upon the earth itself—he'd been trained to properly rest his body to prepare for enemy action.

He *hadn't* been prepared for a curvaceous bluestocking with chestnut eyes, lustrous curls, and a devilishly tempting proposal. Turning her down had been the hardest thing he'd done since leaving the army... until she'd asked him to help unlace her stays. His smallclothes tightened at the memory of his trembling fingers lifting that long, soft hair from the nape of her neck.

Did he find her attractive? Lying naked in the snowdrifts wouldn't cool his ardor. The saving grace was that he wouldn't have to try it. She'd be gone in a few hours.

He swung his feet onto the floor and rolled the kinks from his shoulders. It was morning. The snow would shortly begin to melt. And if not, well, that's why God had invented shovels. People had places to be. The mail coach wouldn't rumble by until noon, but the hack drivers would start rolling past long before. By midday, he'd be back in dreadful solitude.

Then, and only then, would he reenter his bedchamber, lay his head upon warm pillows that still smelled of her perfume, and allow himself to think of what might have been, had the circumstances been different.

But first, he would have to go re-lace the lady. Otherwise, she wouldn't be able to dress at all. He splashed cold water on his face and scowled at his reflection. Perhaps throwing himself upon a snowdrift wasn't such a bad idea.

Why must women's clothing be so... *interactive?*

Xavier could get in and out of full regimentals in a matter of seconds. In fact, he'd let his valet go when he'd joined the army and hadn't bothered to look for a replacement since his return. He didn't need a valet. His retinue of five— a cook, a housekeeper, a butler, a footman, and a stableboy—were more than sufficient for an ex-soldier in a country cottage.

If only his servants were here! The cook and the housekeeper could play lady's maids whilst Xavier and the other three men shoveled snowdrifts all the way back to London if need be.

Of course, if they *were* here, they would constitute five more witnesses to Miss Downing's utter and complete ruin. As it stood now, there was still a chance, however slim, of getting her packed off and back home with everything important intact and no one ever being the wiser.

He dressed quickly. When he tugged on his first boot, his stockinged toes sank into something damp and spongy. He scowled and jerked his foot free. There could only be one explanation. He turned over his Hessian and curled his lip in disgust as a wet clump of cat hair and cravat threads tumbled out.

Egui. The world's smallest, and most efficient, chaperone.

When there was no more personal grooming he could do to procrastinate the inevitable, Xavier made his way down the corridor toward his bedchamber.

Gentle firelight spilled from the open doorway.

She was awake. Of course she was awake. Her cat couldn't have left the bedchamber without her having first opened the door.

He knocked on the doorjamb without peering inside. "Good morning, Miss Downing. You're up early. Did you not sleep well?"

"I usually rise with the sun, though 'tis not very fashionable. Come in, come in. You don't intend to hold a conversation from the other side of a wall, do you?"

He did consider a wall to be the safest of all possible barriers, but he supposed it was the least practical. He rolled back his shoulders and stepped into the open doorway.

His throat dried.

Miss Downing had moved the stool before the fireplace and sat with her back toward him. A cinnamon-colored dress gaped below her nape as she tilted her head to one side and struggled to drag a pearl comb through her long, wavy hair. Each curl glimmered in the firelight, then nestled back against the curve of her breast and the small of her spine.

He had never seen anything more erotic in his life.

"Would you like me to—" He clapped his chest when his voice came out far too husky. After clearing his throat, he tried again. "Shall I lace your stays?"

"Only if you wish to." Rosy firelight—or perhaps a light blush—colored her exposed neck.

"I *have* to," he answered, not bothering to hide the strangled desperation in his voice. "For both of us."

"You don't have to." She turned around and looked him square in the eyes. "You *wish* to."

A surprised laugh burst from his throat. His bluestocking might be exceptionally well read, but she knew very little about men.

"No. What I *wish* to do are acts so unapologetically carnal, the ink would catch fire if I attempted to commit my ideas to paper. But what I'm going to do is lace up your stays, toast some breakfast, and put you on the first coach back to London. You will thank me later."

"I will *think* of you later." The tip of her tongue ran along the bottom of her upper lip. "Just as I did last night."

He clutched the doorjamb and held his position. If he went to her right now, it would not be to lace her stays. They were playing with fire.

She turned back to the hearth and resumed teasing the knots from her curly hair. "I don't suppose you've any skill with a comb? My lady's maid is the only one who could ever vanquish these tangles, and I fear I'm only making the matter worse."

His jaw worked. He was profoundly grateful she couldn't witness the naked desire writ upon his face.

Yes, he wanted to run his fingers through that long, silken hair. To touch it, to comb it, but mostly to have its softness be the sole blanket above their hot, twined bodies.

Which was simultaneously the best and worst idea to have ever crossed his mind. He liked her too much to let her throw away her future on a tryst with someone like him.

"We can't be lovers, Miss Downing. Now or ever. You think me someone I am not." As she met his gaze, he infused his tone with cold finality. "Your vision of me is flawed. A romanticized, idealized knight who saves the day and wins his lady's favor. I am no knight. I do not deserve your favors. I will not be your seducer."

She lifted a half-bare shoulder. "Right now I think you're someone who doesn't know how to unknot curly hair and doesn't wish to come out and say so."

"I know how to comb hair." Against his better judgment, he stormed forward and snatched the pearl comb from her fingers. "Stand up. Not another word until you're properly laced."

She rose to her feet as docile as a lamb.

Xavier wasn't remotely fooled.

With the comb between his teeth, he cinched her stays and buttoned her gown as quickly as possible. When she settled back on the stool, he lifted her hair in one hand and began to gently tease the tangles free, starting from the ends.

The firelight caught each curl as it released, turning the long brown waves into rippling gold.

When a contented little sigh escaped Miss Downing's throat, the tension in his neck muscles softened. Her eyes were closed, and a half-smile curved her lips. The corners of his mouth quirked in response.

His seductive bluestocking was a far better cat than that devil creature she'd brought in a basket. He could comb her hair for hours, just to listen to her relaxed sighs and watch the blissful expression upon her pretty face.

His fingers froze in place. He could do this for *hours?* Just because she liked it?

"Good enough." He tossed the comb into her lap and stalked out the door before her big brown eyes and sweet-smelling skin domesticated him any further. She would be gone in the next two hours. He would see to it personally.

He kicked a fur-speckled pile of what looked like his favorite undershirt out of the middle of the corridor and began to pile on his outerwear. Hat, scarf, coat, gloves. He snatched his shovel from around the corner. Forget the breakfast. He was no innkeeper. He was an irascible, soulless, *solitary* ex-soldier, and the lady was going home. Right. Now.

He swung open the front door. A mountain of snow tumbled inside. It was piled almost as high as the tops of his boots—and still falling. He stared in disbelief.

A thick blanket of white snow covered every inch of the horizon. No, not a blanket. Most blankets weren't ten inches thick and growing. He couldn't distinguish the road from his garden. Everything was white—and impassible. His blood ran cold.

This was a scourge. This was *disaster*. Bloody hell.

Chapter Nine

SNOWBOUND?

Jane wrapped her arms around her chest to keep from flinging them wide and twirling about the parlor in glee. *Snowbound*.

She had been soundly rejected upon her arrival and hadn't yet decided whether the humiliation or the disappointment had hurt more... but this morning's conversation had made it plain that Captain Grey was not immune to her, and—snowbound! She couldn't have planned for a more promising turn of events. There was still a chance!

Of course, if she were to nurture that chance, the first order of business was to improve his terrible mood.

He was understandably less enthusiastic than she was about the ongoing snowstorm. Being trapped in here with him meant his staff was trapped somewhere else, and there were meals to prepare and hearths to stock and cat fur covering most of the cottage.

There wasn't much Jane could do about the abundance of fur or the dearth of firewood, but while Captain Grey was fixing breakfast, she collected the linens Egui had destroyed and safely hid away whatever the cat had not yet found. It might take Captain Grey an extra half hour to find his clean shirts, but at least they would be whole when he did so.

She sat at the dining table and placed three stockings and a waistcoat into her lap. The more unfortunate items were either in dire need of de-furring or had been clawed to shreds, but these were still salvageable. She could darn the stockings and sew new buttons onto the waistcoat before he'd even finish toasting the bread.

Nor was it an unusual morning chore. After so many years with Egui, she not only carried a mending bag at all times, she'd become quite clever at cross-stitch and embroidery. 'Twas the only female "accomplishment" she'd ever found practical. She had yet to be begged to perform critical pianoforte scales or paint an emergency watercolor.

Sewing, at least, gave her something useful to do while Captain Grey was in the kitchen fixing meals. An extra flourish here and there gave her hems a personal touch. And helped to pass the time.

She finished the last of the day's mending just as he emerged from the kitchen. From the set of his jaw, he had no intention of engaging in polite small talk or otherwise passing an agreeable morning in shared companionship.

Jane had no intention of wasting a single second. The snow could melt at any moment, and when it did so, she intended to be… well, if not indispensable, then at least thoroughly ravished.

She had proposed becoming his mistress not because she thought it a likely turn of events, but because it gave her higher ground from which to haggle. Sharing a town house with her brother had taught her that one's starting point very often determined one's outcome.

If Captain Grey said, "I shall not touch you," and Jane begged, "Oh, please, won't you kiss me?" there wasn't much room for compromise. But if Captain Grey said, "I shall not touch you," and Jane suggested, "Why not be lovers?" then perhaps a conciliatory kiss wouldn't be wholly out of the question.

Foremost, however, was getting him to stop glowering at her as if she had orchestrated a seduction *and* the sudden snowstorm.

She took a sip of her tea as she considered the problem. The first step to defuse a male in a wretched mood was to not toss new complaints upon the fire.

"Thank you for preparing breakfast." She ate a third of her toasted bread before meeting his eyes and smiling. "The toast is lovely, and the tea is just what I needed."

He glared back at her without a sound.

Of course he couldn't make a sound. Compliments and *thank you* were incredibly difficult sallies to argue with. She hid her smile. Once he found he could not provoke her into an argument, perhaps they could move on to better topics.

This had to be tough for him. As a soldier—more specifically, a captain—he would be far more accustomed to giving orders than to receiving them. He would not have risen in the ranks so quickly if he had not been a respected, skillful commander every step of the way.

It was not hard to imagine a man as strong and honorable as him leading cavalry into battle or playing mentor to the aspiring officers among his troops. His epaulets and his title spoke to his courage and heroism.

What she was more interested in was the man behind the regimentals. Or rather, beneath them. He had not always been a soldier, and now that the war was over, he found himself facing the unenviable prospect of becoming what he once was: just a man.

Except no man was "just" a man. Everybody carried their unique hopes, dreams, and passions in their hearts. The trick was finding someone who shared them. Or would at least listen.

This was where Jane excelled. She was extremely adept at listening. She nibbled her toast.

This morning was as good a start as any. She *had* to make the most of the situation. If Captain Grey looked at her and thought of carnal acts, plural, then she was determined to try as many as she could before she had to leave.

Her spine straightened. If she was going to be ruined, then by God she wanted to do it right. She wanted hot enough memories to keep her warm for the rest of her lonely, spinster life.

"The expression on your face is quite disturbing," Captain Grey said as he reached for the teapot. "Napoleon was said to look just that way before charging off to conquer a neighboring country."

Jane smiled. Such a statement was obviously meant to nettle, but she didn't rise to the bait. Whether he realized it or not, his disgruntlement now was mostly for show. He'd even refilled her teacup before attending to his own.

"Close enough," she said lightly, lifting her cup to her lips and breathing in the fragrant steam. If she wished for him to warm up to her, she must choose a less incendiary topic than lovemaking. "I was thinking about how difficult it must be to be a soldier and how honorably you must have acquitted yourself in order to earn the rank of captain."

He slammed down the teapot hard enough to crack the handle. "You know nothing of battle and even less about soldiers. Do not romanticize me or the war. *Any* war. 'Tis nothing more than troops of killers murdering other killers in the name of their esteemed leader, who is likely to be far more bloodthirsty than brilliant."

Her mouth fell open. "How can you say that? Napoleon was mad—and, yes, our own king has been deemed unfit to rule—but that does not make the cause you fought for any less worthy. What of Wellington? And the Fifteenth Regiment of Dragoons? I have read countless accounts on all the skirmishes, and—"

"Hearsay," he spat with disgust. "You are proving my point. You know nothing of life if your only knowledge of it comes from books."

Her teeth clenched. He wanted a row? Fine. "Only an ignoramus would claim there's no knowledge to be found in books. Literature may not provide firsthand experience, but reading still has value. Perhaps if the leaders you hate knew their history a little better, war wouldn't break out so easily."

"Battle changes people, Miss Downing. I know you can't understand what that means, but—"

"Why can't I? Because of books again? You might recall that I also interact with *people* upon occasion." She set down her teacup before she threw it at him. "My best friend married *your* best friend, who returned from the selfsame war just as heroic and as honorable as he went in. But you're right. Not everyone did. The privateer sent to rescue Grace's mother had captained a ship in the Royal Navy, fighting Napoleon from the sea. Before enlisting, that man was a *barrister*. So don't tell me I don't understand that war can change people, Captain Grey. I do know. I've seen it. I can also see you."

His chest expanded and he crossed his thick arms before it. "What is that supposed to mean?"

"It means I haven't forgotten who you were before you became what you are now," she said in exasperation. "You and Lord Carlisle and Major Blackpool were intermittently present at the same events and soirées I myself attended. The earl had not yet lost his father. The major had not yet lost his leg and his brother. And you had not yet lost your reason. The fact that you're feeling well enough to argue with me today proves that no matter how the war changed you, *you kept changing*. You're not the empty shell of a man Carlisle dragged through London like an oversize doll. You're you again."

He glared at her in silence.

She lowered her voice. "War is terrible. I recognize that. But now it's over. What happens next is up to you."

He pushed to his feet and piled the dishes and silverware into a stack. "It's not that simple, and we're done talking about it."

She gathered the cups and the teapot and followed him into the kitchen. "Of course it's not simple. Did you know Major Blackpool was one of only two people who ever bothered to stand up to dance with me at a ball? That moment will literally never happen again. He no longer attends balls. He's missing a leg. From what I understand, he can barely walk and shall never dance again. But *his life isn't over.*"

Captain Grey submerged the plates into a bucket of water and pushed it out of her reach. "Who was the other man you danced with?"

"My brother. Why won't you let me wash the dishes?"

"Scullery work is hard on the skin, and you have pretty hands." He began to scrub the first plate. "Blackpool is a hero. I am not. You'd do well to remember that. It would be the height of foolishness to trust a man who doesn't trust himself."

She shook her head. "Fighting for innocents and defending your country is inherently heroic. I believe in you. Closing yourself off won't change that. No matter what you do, your heroism will always—"

He grabbed her face with wet hands and closed his mouth over hers with bruising force. No doubt he expected her to swoon, or slap him, or some other such nonsense.

She gripped his arms and held on tight.

His lips were wide and firm against hers. The rough hands cradling her face dripped with water, but all she felt was warm. Desired. He wasn't simply kissing her. He was holding her in place as if he never wanted to let her go. Hope soared within her. She pressed herself even closer and let her eyes flutter closed.

Even through his clothes, the muscles of his arms were tight and firm beneath her ungloved hands. What would it be like to feel them wrapped around her? Would he hold her close with the same desperate passion that had begun this kiss? Or would his embrace be tender, as his lips were now, brushing against hers with gentle insistence?

As he suckled her lower lip, her mouth parted—not in surprise, but in eagerness. Just because it was her first kiss didn't mean she was ignorant of what pleasures it might bring. She rose on her toes to meet him.

She had researched the matter extensively and was delighted to discover that he had been right about book knowledge failing to communicate the complete picture. No mere words on parchment could remotely convey the heat and immediacy and... *dizziness* of having his mouth mold to hers. The heady sensation of need and shared desire.

Being kissed was more than she'd ever imagined. Being kissed by *him* was more than she'd ever dreamed.

Her fingers trembled—her entire body trembled—and she clutched his neck with abandon. She could no longer stand. She couldn't feel her legs, her knees, anything except her mouth on his and their bodies cleaving together. The rest of the world melted away. It was as if she'd been waiting for this moment, this man, all of her life.

She licked at his lower lip and thrilled when a raw groan escaped his throat. Her heart hammered against her ribs, pushing her bosom against his chest with every staccato beat. All she could think was that she never wanted their kiss to end. This was heaven.

His tongue met hers and a delicious shiver shot down her spine, electrifying her skin. He tasted of tea, but also of a spice she could not define. He tasted of virile man, she supposed. Of Captain Xavier Grey. Everything about him was strong and sure and masculine and completely irresistible. She wanted to be his. She wanted him to be hers.

Her knees weakened. He felt like home and danger and hope all wrapped into one. Her breath escaped in tiny bursts when she remembered to breathe at all. He didn't just make her *feel* desirable. He proved with every consuming kiss, with the thundering of his own heart against hers, that his desire for her was powerful enough to devour them both.

She was already lost.

He pulled away, gasping, and ran a shaking hand through his hair.

It was all she could do not to sway right back into his embrace.

"Was that heroic?" he rasped. "Or was it a selfish man doing what selfish men do?"

She gazed back at him in wonder. Her lips were tender from his kiss. "It was beautiful."

"It was foolish." He turned back to the bucket and reached for the next dirty saucer. "It shan't be repeated."

Chapter Ten

IT WAS ALL Xavier could do not to stick his head in the bucket of soapy water and drown himself for being such an imbecile.

Was grabbing Miss Downing and kissing her meant to teach her a *lesson* of some sort? What pearl of wisdom, precisely, had he intended to impart, other than if the snow didn't ease up soon, he was going to have to build an impenetrable ice hut and encase himself inside?

He supposed he'd meant to prove that he was not an honorable man, nor a wise object upon which to pin one's cap. A smart man would not have kissed her. An honorable man absolutely would not have done.

Why couldn't she see that by dubbing him "hero" of this charade, he would prove himself unheroic with the mere acceptance of the role?

Heaven knew he'd been unheroic enough to last a lifetime. When he'd realized he could not be trusted around others, he had sunk to the most desperate of solutions. At first, he'd shuttered himself inside his mind. When that proved unsustainable—curse the empathy of true friends!— he'd managed to shutter himself in a tiny cottage, a solid mile from the nearest posting house.

Then *she* came along. And he'd kissed her.

The smart thing to do—the *only* thing to do— was to be heroic enough for them both. If she would not watch out for her best interests, he would have to work twice as hard. Thrice as hard. Oh, God, was he ever hard...

He groaned. If he was ever to acquit himself in some small way, she must retain her innocence. And obviously, it was up to him to ensure that happened. Miss Downing was unlikely to assist him in his mission to preserve her chastity.

She seemed to believe his home a fortress of anonymity, within which all depraved acts could be wantonly enjoyed without a soul ever becoming the wiser. As if she believed whatever happened in the captain's cottage, stayed in the captain's cottage.

Naïve beyond all reckoning. He shook his head. There were no such things as secrets.

He had staff that would arrive as soon as the roads were passable. She had servants—and a brother—who would at some point wonder what had become of her. If there weren't likenesses nailed to every wall across England already. And of course, she had yet to make it home without calling attention to her adventure. He grimaced. Good Lord.

Even if he outfitted her with a chastity belt and a wimple, hundreds of people would cross her path between Chelmsford and London. People with eyes, ears, and wagging tongues. The only chance that remained of returning her home with her reputation intact was to ensure there was little reason to doubt it. Starting with never learning she'd crossed his door.

He must resume his scheme of converting her image of him into one of a mere acquaintance. It had to work. One did not seduce one's acquaintances. While she was here, he and Miss Downing would adhere to what was proper. They'd be nothing less and nothing more than perfectly dull, perfectly *respectable*... friends.

But guarding a young lady's reputation required more than merely abstaining from making love to her. Especially with a woman as unconventional and unpredictable as this one.

Even without succumbing to carnal pleasures, there was nothing maiden-appropriate with which to pass the time. He was a bachelor. This was his home. Very little within its walls was appropriate for a young lady. She shouldn't be anywhere near him or the dishes. Zeus. What was he to do?

He didn't even own a backgammon set. Yet he must ensure their one hundred percent platonic friendship didn't degenerate to her swilling whiskey and smoking cigarillos as she tossed betting markers across a velvet card table. His cottage must remain a citadel of respectability.

Which left what? Organizing his linen closet?

Excitement rushed through his veins. No, not his linen closet. His *library*. What could be safer than a room full of books?

His chest lightened. He washed the last of the dishes and dried his hands on a towel. A library like his could take weeks to organize. He didn't even know what was on the shelves. He'd purchased titles at whim and left them helter-skelter when he'd set off for war.

With luck, the volumes were so dusty that they'd cause sneezing fits every time they were touched. No man was less kissable than whilst suffering a violent coughing attack.

He proffered his arm. "Would you like to see my library?"

Her lips curved, but she narrowed her eyes in mock suspicion. "Dare I hope for a prurient collection of *shunga* scrolls?"

He took a step back. "I am delighted to say that I have no idea what that means."

She laughed. "Why would you be happy about that?"

He fixed her with an imperious stare. "Whatever it is, I doubt it is something proper."

"Who would want a *proper* library?" Her eyes widened and she tilted her head. "Don't tell me you're one of those pretentious sorts who only purchases books with the hope of impressing callers with their size or title."

"I never meant to show anyone my library, so, no, I am not so lowly a creature as that. However, I haven't laid eyes on my books in well over three years, and I couldn't begin to tell you what I might have thought worth perusing at that time. Essays on irrigation methods? Travel journals? French poetry? I imagine there's a few of everything upon those shelves."

She hesitated, clearly tempted. "I recognize this as a blatant attempt to avoid other outlets for amusement."

"And yet you cannot resist." He turned her toward the door and offered his arm once more. "What if the snow should melt by noontime? You might never get another chance to discover the hidden secrets of a captain's library."

She slapped her hand onto the crook of his arm in resignation. "You don't fight fair."

"You don't know the half of it," he said quietly. He hoped she never would.

She released his arm when they reached the library and preceded him into the room. He followed close behind. As soon as he entered, she pulled the door closed behind them.

He arched a sardonic brow. "Was the empty cottage not private enough, madam?"

She arched a brow right back. "Have you met my cat?"

His gaze jerked to his shelves in horror. It was one thing for his books to be dusty… and quite another for them to be a pulpy, fur-sodden mess.

Fortunately, all seemed to be in order. Perhaps too much in order. All the titles were upright and even, with nary a cobweb to be found.

Curse his competent staff.

Miss Downing began a slow examination of the room. Xavier lit a small fire with his flint and then settled onto the chaise longue to watch.

She wasn't just beautiful. Everything about her was bewitching and larger than life. Her huge brown eyes. Her mane of wild, curly hair. Her pouty lips and curvaceous figure. Her literate, clever mind. The sheer force of her will. Her single-minded intensity. How seductively she walked. How sweetly she kissed.

He gritted his teeth. This was Operation Platonic Friendship. He was not to think about the taste of her mouth or the sway of her hips.

They needed to spend the entirety of the day discussing Wordsworth and Voltaire. Or rather, something less… provocative. He didn't want to make a good impression. Perhaps he ought to engage her in a lively debate on whether library books were best catalogued by size or color.

"What do you think of my collection?" he found himself asking instead.

"Well…" She poked her head from around a corner. "The topics are varied enough, but at least half have never been read. The pages aren't even sliced."

"You can do the honors, if you've found something you'd like to read." He adjusted a small pillow and stretched out upon the chaise longue. He didn't much care who sliced the pages, but if offering her the privilege made him seem like a good friend, he'd be happy to lend his knife.

Eyes sparkling, she bounced in place. "I can read anything that I want?"

"As long as it isn't..." He hesitated. What had she mentioned earlier? Sugar? Shogun? "...*shunga* scrolls."

The corners of her mouth quirked. "Nobody reads *shunga* scrolls. They just look at the pictures."

He cut her a flat look.

She gave an innocent flutter of eyelashes and selected a book from the shelves. "Lie back down. I'll read something to you. How about the *Odyssey* in original Greek?"

He couldn't even remember purchasing it. "Do you mind if I snore?"

"I hope you do. But I'll translate aloud in case you manage to stay awake." Rather than take another chair, she perched at the foot of the chaise longue with her back toward him. "Ahem. Page the first. '*Tell me, O muse, of that ingenious hero...*'"

There. Xavier relaxed his head against the cushion. Nothing could be more respectable.

Or less stimulating. He hadn't actually intended to snore, but neither had he anticipated the level of mortal dullness in which Miss Downing read aloud. She could not have infused less life into her tone had she merely been counting sheep.

He might have told her not to bother translating since it wasn't doing either of them any favors, except he saw no advantage to being rude. His goal was to be perceived as a friend, not the enemy. Enemies could incite passion.

Miss Downing's monotone could only incite slumber.

After a while, he let his eyelids drift closed. It had been a long, cold night filled with nothing but vivid waking dreams. He had been exhausted from the moment he rolled out of bed. Her tone was pacifying in its relentless uniformity, the words forgettable and relaxing.

He *almost* didn't notice when she skipped from Calypso to Circe in the space of a breath. Her low words droned on without hitch. His eyes flew open. How could she have turned thirty pages at once without noticing? How could she have skipped the *Trojan horse* without noticing?

Sleep forgotten, he propped himself up on one elbow to glance over her shoulder at the text.

And roared. "What the *devil* are you reading, woman?"

She jumped, her cheeks flushing a rosy pink. "You said I might read whatever I wished."

"You said you were reading the *Odyssey*!"

"I said I would read *you* the *Odyssey*." She motioned him back to his pillow. "*I'm* reading something else."

"That's not 'something else.'" Heart galloping, he reached for the book.

She held it aloft with her other hand. "You can't have it. I'm right in the middle."

"Absolutely not," he ground out. "That's *The Memoirs of Fanny Hill*, and it's not fit for human eyes."

Her brows arched. "Then why do you have it?"

"Because I'm inhuman! Give me the damn book or I'll—"

"Oh, lie back down. You were almost asleep. I've already read most of what you're afraid of, so there's not much harm in reading the rest."

He collapsed back against the chaise and covered his face with his hands. No wonder the woman's storytelling abilities had been execrable. She'd been quoting from memory whilst reading an entirely different story. One in which an innocent country miss was procured by a bawdyhouse madam and then descended into a life of erotic abandon.

"What part are you at now?" he rasped, his throat dry.

"Mmm. Fanny is peering through closet curtains at the proprietress's boudoir. This is after she spent the night in the same bed as Phoebe. How that girl failed to guess Phoebe's trade as a whore after the woman kissed her and stroked her and brought her almost to the edge of relief is completely beyond all credulity."

Xavier kept his hands over his eyes and groaned. He, too, could recite a few literary passages from memory. Not one of them was appropriate for platonic friendships.

"I'm now at the part where Fanny espies an erect male member for the very first time." Miss Downing's voice turned conspiratorial. "I can certainly understand her excitement and curiosity, as I haven't had the pleasure myself."

Lord save him. He moaned into his hands. Things had somehow got even worse. His mission hadn't failed after all. Instead, he had accidentally become the-friend-to-which-she-shared-all-erotic-secrets. Platonic was worse than lovers. Platonic was hell.

"Here, I'll read the next part. See if you remember it." The chaise creaked as she straightened her spine and took a deep breath. This time, her voice was low and throaty, as rich and seductive as wine.

"*The madam's sturdy stallion had now unbuttoned, and produced naked, stiff and erect, that wonderful machine, which I had never seen before, and which, for the interest my own seat of pleasure began to take furiously in it, I stared at with all the eyes I had…"'*

He sprang upright, snatched the novel from her fingers, and hurled it across the room.

His bluestocking glared at him in high fury. "Must you be so vexing, Captain Crotchety? I was just getting to the good part."

"You want to know the good parts?" he exploded. "Fanny watches them rut, is aroused, brings herself to pleasure, spies on yet another trysting couple, becomes overset with lust, and throws herself at the first lone male she comes across. There. It's spoiled. There's no point in reading it." He leaped to his feet and yanked her to hers. "No more library. I might have a chess set somewhere. We're going to play a nice respectable game of chess even if we're missing a few pieces. I'll whittle new ones if I have to."

"You don't have to be so disagreeable," she muttered, shaking her arm free from his grip.

Oh, yes, he did. It was either disagreeable or naked, and he was perilously close to choosing the latter.

He locked the library door securely behind them and turned his back on the maddening, stimulating, delectable Miss Downing. His blood raced just from looking at her. He wasn't abstaining from seduction for his sake, but for hers.

It was the only thread of decency he had left.

Chapter Eleven

XAVIER MANAGED TO AVOID all conversation with Miss Downing until late that afternoon when his stomach growled its displeasure. If he was hungry, she must be hungry. And the snow had yet to cease.

He sighed. They would have to share another meal. Anything else would be impractical. He might as well start cooking.

It was bad enough that his army-honed culinary skills were better suited for a dungeon. Now they'd have to nibble sliced cheese and roasted vegetables while phrases like *stiff and erect* and *she pleasured herself* still hung between them.

He ran a hand over his face. He'd thought that his primary attraction to the unstoppable Miss Downing was the very fact of her untouched innocence. Of her managing to be something good and true and pure in a world of war and deception and hate.

Over and over, she'd proven him wrong. Yes, she was both a virgin and good-natured, as expected. She was also clever, confident, and un-apologetically sensual. In other words... the perfect woman. For someone else. He swallowed hard.

If only he could stop *wanting* her so bloody much.

He attacked the cheese with a knife as the vegetables roasted over a fire. Supper wouldn't be much, but it would be edible.

Three years of hell had taught Xavier never to rely on anyone else's assistance. Even without his cook present, Xavier's larder was stocked with enough provisions to keep a non-finicky bachelor fed through springtime. Including a hidden stash of the sweets he'd missed so much while he'd been away.

A young lady like Miss Downing, however, would keep to a higher standard. The back of his neck heated as he realized she might be disappointed in his meager offerings. She must be used to more. *Deserved* more. But until the snow stopped falling, all she got was him.

To her credit, she voiced no complaints. They even made it through most of the meal without a single mention of inappropriate topics. But as his sultry houseguest popped the last of the after-dinner sweetmeats into her mouth, she fixed her gaze on his with a slow smile.

For the first time in his life, he wished he were a candied pear.

She licked her lips and reached for her glass of wine. "Is the library still restricted?"

"Absolutely." Every single part of him was feeling restricted, just from watching her tongue moisten those plump red lips. He ground his teeth. Perhaps he ought to open the library back up and lock her inside until morning. "Also forbidden are bed play, whiskey, cheroots, gambling, and eighteenth-century erotica."

"Everything fun, you mean." She gave him a teasing pout.

He willed his body not to respond.

"If we're to entertain ourselves without any physical activities," she continued, "then we'll have to make do with conversation. Since we're snowbound at the moment, surely you cannot object to getting to know each other a little better over another glass of wine?"

God's teeth. "One glass was enough."

The corners of her mouth twitched. "A cup of milk, then. We can even sit on opposite sides of the parlor."

"Fine." Milk sounded good. Milk sounded *innocent*. "Go sit. I'll join you as soon as I clear the table."

"I can help with the—"

"Go pick your side of the parlor."

She laughed under her breath, but she rose to her feet with good grace and sashayed away.

He gathered the dishes and deposited them in a bucket of clean water in the kitchen. The current supply of fresh water would barely cover scullery duties and separate baths for him and the lady. The next time he took the cat out for a walk, he'd have to remember to bring in more snow.

Good. He could use a nice long tromp outside in the cold to help him forget about the nice warm woman he'd left inside.

She was seated in one of two wingback chairs when he entered the parlor. Both chairs were positioned at complementary angles such that they somewhat faced the fire, and somewhat faced each other—without either occupant being forced to stare in either direction. Not precisely opposite sides of the parlor, but at least they wouldn't be sharing the sofa.

"So." He dropped onto the unoccupied chair and stretched out his feet. "Sagittarius?"

Her mouth fell open. "You cannot possibly follow astrology."

"I cannot possibly," he agreed. At least they wouldn't be discussing the stars. "Have you a better jumping off point for making light conversation under awkward conditions?"

"I do." The sugary sweetness in her tone raised the hair on the back of his neck. She tapped the tips of her fingers together and smiled. "I thought we might play *Boon or Bare*."

His muscles tensed. "Boon or *what?*"

Her brown eyes laughed at him from beneath their curled lashes. "I presume you've never been a twelve-year-old girl?"

The Captain's Bluestocking Mistress   111

He arched his brows at her in silence.

She winked back. "It's a game of twenty questions, goose. To which you bare your soul, not your derrière, in case that's what has you all bothered. Should you choose to not answer a question, you owe the asker the boon of their choice." She relaxed against her chair, her gaze sparkling with challenge. "I cannot credit that a big strong captain would be afraid of a game little girls play when they spend the night with their cousins."

Famous. He glared at her sourly. He could see where this was going.

If she earned a boon, she was going to ask for another kiss... or she'd head straight for the fireworks. But since the only other activities in his snowbound bachelor home were worse than this silly game, he was out of better options for entertainment.

He rolled the kinks out of his shoulders. Exhausted as he was, he would have to stay *en garde*. He wanted to keep her out of trouble. *She* wanted a glimpse inside his brain. Or his breeches. He shifted his weight as a shiver slid down his back. The easiest way to avoid owing boons would be to just answer her questions.

Somehow, that was more frightening.

"Five," he bit out. "You get five questions, not twenty."

"We get five questions," she corrected. Victory lit her from within, making her even more beautiful. "Do you wish to start, or shall I?"

Perhaps he should've allowed twenty. The longer he could string out idle conversation, the less trouble they'd get into. He waved his fingers with as much careless disdain as he could muster. "Ladies first."

As she leaned forward, her eyes turned serious. "If we're both attracted to each other, why do you refuse to act on it?" Her pulse fluttered at her throat. "I'm not looking for forever. Just lovemaking. No one will even know."

"Because you *should* be looking for forever." He ran jerky fingers through his hair. So much for idle conversation. *One* question was too many. Well, if she wasn't going to let the topic drop, the best thing to do was tell the truth. Perhaps that would shake some sense into her. "It's never 'just lovemaking.' When you do choose a man, your relationship should be something you're both proud of. Seek commitment, not secrecy. Promise me you'll never settle for someone unwilling to proclaim his love for you from every rooftop in London."

She frowned. "But I'm not looking for love."

"Aren't you?"

Her mouth tightened. "Is that your first question?"

He lifted his brows. "It's one you should be asking yourself."

She stabbed a finger in his direction. "You haven't answered mine. You've informed me why I shouldn't have *my* viewpoint, but what I asked for is yours."

His muscles tightened. He hated this game already. If it had ever been just a game. He drummed his fingers on his armrests. Now that he'd agreed to play, he intended to keep his word. Even if he'd rather take her cat for long walks in the snow than struggle to put feelings into words.

"Separating what I should do from what you should do isn't as simple as you seem to think," he said at last. "You *are* a marriageable young lady. You *are* still a virgin. You *are* good at heart. By taking your innocence, I would rob you of the opportunity to find someone who *is* worthy of you."

She leaned forward. "But I—"

"You asked what *I* thought." He took a deep breath and let the words come as they may. This was the time for truth, not eloquence. "Your maidenhead isn't something you can get back once you've lost it. No matter what terms you think you're offering, accepting those terms would be taking advantage of your innocence. I won't rob you of your future. I ruined more than enough lives in Belgium. Don't ask me to be a monster in the sanctuary of my own home."

Her lips pressed into a thin line, but she made no further interruption.

Not that it mattered. He was done talking. Every word he'd spoken was true. There was nothing left to say.

She lowered her eyes and lifted her fingers in his direction. "Your question, Captain."

There was only one worth asking. His hands curled into fists. "Your brother is a shite guardian. How the devil did you get here without anyone noticing?"

A flush crept over her cheeks. She didn't like the question? Good. He hoped she regretted tricking him into this farce. If he had to answer questions, so did she.

Still blushing, she met his gaze. "Grace had mentioned you had a cottage outside of Chelmsford. I figured it couldn't be that hard to find. Everyone in a ten-mile radius was bound to know the direction of a decorated army captain."

Splendid. To save her reputation, all they had to do was erase the memories of everyone in a ten-mile radius. Or did they?

"That's how you found my cottage," he said when she didn't continue. "How did you slip away? I cannot believe your brother would give you permission to make this journey, much less unaccompanied."

She worried her lower lip. "Isaac had an important business meeting to attend to, so I was left alone. So I let my lady's maid have a holiday. Don't look so stormy! A woman of four-and-twenty is perfectly capable of taking care of her-self."

Xavier coughed. "Obviously."

"Well, that's how it happened. My brother wasn't home, so I left and came here. It doesn't make him a shite guardian. It just means he trusts me."

"I stand corrected," he drawled. "His wisdom knows no bounds."

Her arms crossed. "Unlike you, Isaac trusts me to do what's right for *me*. My brother wouldn't be happy to learn I snuck off to meet a man, but he wouldn't make snippy little comments about it like a missish harpy."

He'd gone from Captain Crotchety to "missish harpy" in less than an hour, and there was only one explanation: She was absolutely mad.

He took a deep breath and let the subject drop. No matter what he thought of her plan, a great deal of courage had been required to make an unplanned pilgrimage to Chelmsford and risk rejection, humiliation, and ruin. He'd already rejected her. There was no call to add to the hurt.

Especially not when he was trying to be friends.

"Very well," he said quietly. "I didn't mean to be judgmental. I'm just used to being alone."

She leaned forward eagerly. "Is that why you think love is so important?"

"Who said I—?"

"It's obvious. And it's my question." She batted her eyelashes at his clenched jaw, as if trying to tease him out of a foul humor. "Play the game. Why do you feel love is so important?"

He slowly let out his breath. Did he? It sounded so idealistic, and yet... Perhaps it was true.

"I didn't think much of love at first. Not until I realized I was no longer worthy of it." He turned his face toward the fire. "Things have a funny way of gaining importance once they're out of one's grasp." He pinned her with his gaze. "Some say love is a gift. It's also something you earn. Something you deserve or don't deserve, at times through no fault or merit of your own. It's something worth fighting for. Perhaps even dying for. It is often the sole difference between heaven and hell."

Her smile softened. "You're a romantic."

"I'm a cynic. Ravenwood's the one who has always spouted romantic nonsense about marrying for love, ever since the rest of us were old enough to start thinking of young ladies as prizes to win. It was no surprise that he longed for love. He inherited his dukedom when he was eight years old and the estate fell into strange hands. If the coffers weren't restored by the time he came of age, the best he could have hoped for was an heiress."

Her eyes widened. "But he didn't marry for love. He hasn't married at all."

"He doesn't have to. The dukedom is strong again. He can believe love to be as important as he pleases." Xavier shrugged and arched a brow. "Why don't *you* think so?"

She clasped her hands and brought them to her lips in silence.

Not a problem. He was very good at patience. It was his talent, and his curse.

After a moment, she lowered her hands to her lap. "That's your question?"

"It is."

"Then I must answer." But she turned toward the fire and stared at the orange flames leaping behind the grate rather than respond.

He watched in silence. Her discomfort was palpable. Honesty was a very dangerous game indeed.

"I do believe in love," she said at last, without looking at him. "I find it devastatingly important. I just don't think it possible for everyone to find it, and certainly not for me." She lifted her chin. "There's little sense holding out hope for something that's not going to happen. I'm no quixotic dreamer. That's why I'm here. I wanted something more within my grasp." Her eyes glittered in the firelight. "On our way to the opera, I saw elegant courtesans. Penny whores. Fishwives. They all had lovers. And I thought… Why not me?"

"Miss Downing, you are no fishwife. Your lack of husband has nothing to do with—"

"Why did you become a soldier?" she interrupted.

"What?" A laugh startled out of him at the abrupt change in topic. "Why did you become a bluestocking?"

"It's not your turn yet," she snapped.

He blinked and settled back against his chair. They were apparently through discussing love. Or bluestockings. "That's your question?"

"Yes." She leaned back against her chair. "Why did you join the army? The real answer. Not just 'duty' or 'honor.' Why did you truly join?"

His initial reaction was to grind out that duty and honor were reasons as valid as any, but he took a moment to consider the question. Were those *his* reasons? Were they anyone's?

He thought back. "Gossip rags would indicate that otherwise sensible women cannot resist a man in regimentals, but the truth is that little boys cannot resist wishing to *be* that man."

She lifted a hand to her mouth to hide her smile. "You read gossip rags?"

He flashed a rakish grin. "Can I answer that question instead?"

"No, no." She fluttered her fingers. "Carry on with your explanation. Regimentals are universally appealing..."

He inclined his head. "As is the *idea* of honor and duty. Who doesn't wish to be honorable, or at least to be perceived as such? Who doesn't long for the respect of his peers and the adulation of female hearts? When my closest friends purchased their commissions in the King's Army, there was absolutely no question about whether I'd join them. We were invincible, and we were off to become heroes."

"And you did," she said with a smile.

"Did we?" he asked, his voice dry. "Perhaps Carlisle did. I didn't. The rest of us…" His voice trailed off. None of it had worked out as any of them had hoped. "Ravenwood's dukedom kept him from going, and the bullet in Edmund Blackpool's chest kept him from coming back. Go ask Bart how much adulation he's received since returning home without a leg. Even the magic of an officer's regimentals has its limits."

She lifted her chin. "That doesn't mean he's not a hero."

"A hero who can't stand his own reflection." Xavier lifted a shoulder. "Not that I'm overly fond of mine. Is it my turn yet?"

Pensive, she nodded slowly. "Yes. Ask anything you like."

He rubbed his temples. The ability to be clever escaped him at the moment. His head was still brimming with memories of war and the loss and disappointments all his friends had faced. But she'd inadvertently given him a topic to explore.

"What made you become a bluestocking?" he asked. "The real answer. Not just 'I like books.'"

She laughed. "Nobody *chooses* to become a bluestocking, any more than they choose to become a wallflower."

"Nobody?"

She stared at him as if she'd never considered the idea before. Perhaps she hadn't. She chewed her lower lip. "I suppose I *did*. Choose to be a bluestocking, I mean. Not a wallflower. I have tried so hard to make an—but that wasn't the question. Bluestockings. My mother was one. And I wanted to be just like her. She and Aunt Montagu were my heroes."

His elbow slipped off its armrest. "Elizabeth Montagu was your aunt? How could you *not* have become a bluestocking? She fairly invented the practice!"

Miss Downing gazed at the fire. "I think she was perhaps a second or third cousin, several times removed. A fair percentage of the volumes in my private library came from her. I was far too young to attend the literary assemblies, but my mother had done, and she could quote to me from memory."

He couldn't even imagine. "How did your father feel about that?"

"Papa? He was a respected scholar and had once held an advisory position of some renown with the war office. Neither Isaac nor I can recall a time when we weren't surrounded by books and actively reading. In fact, I memorized the *Odyssey* to compete with my brother." She smiled at the memory. "In my family, knowledge was the highest goal one could pursue. 'Bluestocking' wasn't a slur, but rather a term of pride."

In *her* family. An empty feeling gathered in the pit of his stomach. "When did you realize that wasn't true in all families?"

Her mouth tightened. "The day I made my curtsey. Novels weren't shunned in my home any more than periodicals, so between scandal sheets and gothic serials, I was convinced that no matter what happened on the night of my come-out, for better or for worse, it would be absolutely memorable."

"And what happened?"

Her smile didn't reach her eyes. "Nothing."

He frowned. "How could *nothing* happen? If you had a come-out, then certainly *something—*"

"I believe we're overdue for my turn at question-asking." Her voice trembled, then pushed on. "When you first came home from war, you were a hairsbreadth away from vegetative. It took months for you to show any awareness or interest in the world around you."

His spine stiffened. "Is that a question?"

"I'll rephrase." Her stare turned piercing. "Why did you retreat into your own mind?"

He glared at her. "It was safer."

She didn't look away.

Neither did he.

She sighed and held up her palms. "Care to elaborate?"

Not particularly. But nor did he wish to owe her a boon. "No one returns from war the same man he was when he started." He, more than anyone. "I didn't like who I had become. And I couldn't make myself forget."

"Who did you become?"

He shook his head. "That's a different question."

"You lost your innocence," she guessed.

His lips twisted. "I lost that years before."

"I don't mean your virginity. I mean your *innocence*. You thought the world was one way, and it turned out to be another."

"That's... an understatement." It had turned out to be a living hell.

"Earlier, you mentioned that once one loses one's innocence, it cannot be regained." She tilted her head. "That's true. But it's not the whole story."

He stared down at his boots. "Nothing is ever the whole story."

"I mean, as people, we're always losing our innocence about something, aren't we? That doesn't negate or even minimize it, but it does mean we have to keep moving forward." Her lips pursed as she considered him. "You didn't like who you had become. That's fair. But you're no longer that person. That was the old you. This is the new you."

He snorted. "How do you know who or how I am?"

"Because you're not on the battlefield anymore." Her words sped faster. "You say war changes a man. I believe you. But it's not the only thing that changes a person. Who we are at any given moment is a combination of our past experiences, present situation, and potential future. It's not stagnant. The person you no longer liked wasn't the same bright-eyed recruit who joined, or the man you became when you came home."

"A vegetable," he said wryly.

She shook her head. "Not a vegetable. A man searching for answers. I don't know if you found any. Perhaps there are none to find. But whatever you had become, you no longer are. No one is ever the person they were even six months prior. The mere fact of disliking what you'd become inherently changed you for the better."

He ran a hand over his face, then let his head fall back against the chair. "I don't feel better."

"Another sign that you're human. Soldiers protect the greater good. The acts they're called to perform are unpleasant, but their hearts are in the right place."

"Don't both sides think so?" He rubbed the bridge of his nose. How he wished the experience had merely been *unpleasant*.

Her brow wrinkled in concern. "Are you... sympathizing with Napoleon?"

"I'm condemning war in general." He massaged the back of his neck. "And now it's my turn to ask a question."

Her lips scrunched as if she were physically holding herself back from pressing further, but she nodded and lifted a hand for him to continue.

Splendid. Now if only he had a question. Mostly he hadn't wanted to discuss the war, much less his feelings about it. Curse this game. The good news was that she only had one question left. The bad news was that he still had two to go.

At least... it should've felt like bad news. When they'd sat down to play what he'd assumed was frivolous nonsense, there weren't many things he'd wished to do less. But somehow, the fire had dwindled without him noticing.

What had begun as a silly challenge was now a very real, very personal conversation. He found himself not wishing to "waste" questions on trivial topics. Miss Downing was clever and insightful and utterly impossible, and he wanted to know everything about her.

He leaned forward. "My circle of friends is infamous, but I know nothing about yours. Who are your closest friends?"

"Books." She tapped herself on the chest. "Bluestocking, remember?"

Her flippancy surprised him. "I asked a real question."

"I gave a real answer."

"A one-word answer." What had she said to him earlier? He held his palms wide. "Care to elaborate?"

No, she didn't look as though she did. Her arms were folded beneath her chest and her gaze was on the ebbing fire. But then she raised her eyes to his.

"My brother has his own responsibilities to deal with. Grace is married. I'll see her at the Theatre Royal in less than a fortnight for *Cymon*, but we'll be paying attention to the stage, not each other. I have no other family or friends. Which leaves... books." She paused.

He watched her in silence.

"I love books." She smiled in the direction of their feet. "I truly do. They may not love me back, but it feels like they do while I'm reading them. Spending the afternoon with a favorite character gives me more time with someone than I usually get in a month. Before I met Grace, books were the best and only friends I'd had for years. So I spend all the time with them that I can."

"Until now," he said softly.

Her laugh was humorless. "Until I turned up on your doorstep without my library in tow?"

"No." He kept his voice was low and warm. "Apart from Lady Carlisle, the characters you read about were your only friends... until now. Now you have me, too."

Firelight splashed across her startled face.

The back of his neck heated. Embarrassed, he waved a hand. "Your turn. Last question."

Contemplative, she returned her gaze to the fire. When she spoke, her words were so soft he could barely hear them. But he couldn't escape them.

"What precisely occurred to disillusion you and make you believe you had crossed from good to evil?"

His spine went rigid. "I didn't 'believe' it. It's a fact. And I do not deserve forgiveness."

She shook her head. "That's not an answer."

"You won't get an answer."

"Then you owe me a boon."

His muscles tightened. Famous. He could either divulge his darkest regret or open himself up to making new ones. "The boon can't be lovemaking, or forcing me to answer a question I already refused to answer."

She leaned back in her chair. "You don't get to decide the boon or the question. You simply answer, or not."

His heartbeat sped in frustration. He rubbed his temples. "What's your boon, Miss Downing?"

She met his eyes. "Jane."

He blinked. "What?"

"My name is Jane. Now that we're friends, I ask for leave to call you Xavier."

His stomach fluttered. "First-naming each other is your boon?"

She smiled back at him sweetly. "If that's too intimate, we can always try the lovemaking instead."

"My turn to ask a question," he said quickly. She was incorrigible. He couldn't help but grin back at her. *"Jane."*

Her cheeks flushed becomingly.

He angled toward her. "You explained how you got here. *Why* did you do it? You're intelligent enough to realize illicit affairs aren't romantic. They're illicit, and then they're over."

She exhaled slowly. "Perhaps for you, liaisons are illicit and then they're over. I don't have affairs at all."

Xavier doubted that was for lack of interest. Jane was exquisite to look at and only became more beautiful whenever she opened her mouth and spoke.

Her thumb teased her lower lip. "I'm not a wallflower because it's diverting. I'm a wallflower because nobody notices me. I slip through their minds before I can finish reminding them of my name." She wrapped her arms about her chest. "I try to make it a game, to say or do things impossible to ignore. But even at my most outrageous, I never earn a second glance."

Impossible. He would never be able to put her out of his mind.

She looked away. "In truth, I hate society events. I'm invisible in every crowd. It's torture. I can barely sit through an orchestra performance despite my love of violins above all instruments, because every such outing is wrapped inside an hour or three of ignominy. And no one will notice but me. Almack's is even worse."

He pushed to his feet. "Get up."

"What?" She blinked up at him in confusion.

He held out his hand. "Come here."

She placed her hand tentatively in his. "Why?"

"We're dancing." He coaxed her up from her chair.

She glanced over her shoulder at the dimly lit parlor. "Right here?"

"Right. Here." And he pulled her into his arms.

Chapter Twelve

JANE COULDN'T BREATHE.

She'd lost all control of her lungs—and her wobbly legs—the moment Captain Grey pulled her to him. The moment *Xavier* welcomed her into his embrace.

He wanted to dance. How could they dance? There was no music. She couldn't even feel her knees. Not with her hand in his and his other arm about her waist, holding her close. She closed her eyes. He smelled of sandalwood and citrus. Everything about him was rock hard and hot to the touch.

"Know any danceable melodies?" he murmured into her ear.

She shook her head, disappointed. Their dance was over before it began. "I'm afraid my savant abilities are limited to literature."

To her surprise, he began to hum and guided her in time with the rhythm.

She tilted her head to the side and followed his lead. Why was the song so familiar? She was certain she'd heard the melody before. From a violin, perhaps. It almost sounded like... Her breath caught as she recognized the tune.

"It's from *Antigona*." She gazed up at him shyly. "The opera we saw together."

He smiled. "I wanted to dance with you then, too."

Her throat dried. Could it be true? Doubtful. Her gaze fell. It didn't matter. He was being nice. All they would share was this moment. She didn't realize how badly she would long for more.

The muscles beneath his coat tightened as he led her in smooth, graceful circles. She didn't need music to feel like she was floating. The soft firelight made the room all the more romantic. She could almost believe herself the belle of a ball.

Except, fairy tales didn't happen to her. Her fingers grew cold. He was right. Love affairs— even stolen kisses—weren't as carefree as she'd believed. Once the snow was gone, he would forget her just like all the others. And this time, it would break her heart.

"Jane. Look at me." He slipped a knuckle beneath her chin and raised her gaze to his. "I notice you. I see you. I have you in my arms."

Her lips parted and her eyes stung. Until he'd spoken the words, she hadn't realized that she'd been waiting for them her entire life.

With nothing more than a soft murmur, he'd carved open her soul and left a part of himself inside. She would never be the same. Her heart clattered at an alarming rate, but she could not look away. Nor did she wish to.

His gorgeous blue eyes shone from beneath inky lashes. The intensity of his gaze was thrilling and frightening and filled her with wonder.

He saw her. Plump, boring Jane. And yet he still wanted her in his arms.

When they completed their circuit about the room, he paused before the fireplace—but did not immediately release her.

She hoped he never would. The evening had been magical. *He* was magical. She would be happy to stay right here, wrapped in his arms, forever. But all she had was this moment.

He lowered his head to hers. His lips grazed her cheekbone, her earlobe, the pulse point just beneath the line of her jaw. Her heart fluttered. Was he finally giving in to their chemistry? Or was he acting out of pity?

She angled her head, seeking his mouth. She wanted to feel his lips against hers. To have him and taste him, and to know that this time, he wasn't kissing her because she was bothersome. He'd be kissing her because he wanted her. Because he saw her. Because he *liked* her.

When his mouth caught hers, gooseflesh rippled along her skin, followed by an infusion of molten desire. Her hot flesh ached to be free of her clothing so that she could feel her body even more intimately against his. Her heart thundered. Perhaps he would finally make love to her.

She slid her hands up his strong arms to his neck, where overlong black hair curled against the stark white of his cravat, and kissed him back. He was wonderful.

He noticed her. He saw that she *wished* to be seen. He made her believe that forever was something she actually deserved. She melted against him. He wouldn't kiss her like this unless he felt it, too. Unless he *meant* it, at least for this moment. No one else looked outside of themselves long enough to wonder what torture others might be going through. No one else reached deep into the furthest crevices of her heart and dared to ask, why *not* love? Why not her, too?

His lips were firm and warm. The dance of his tongue against hers, exhilarating. Her heart swelled. When she'd set out on this journey, she'd assumed the lustful nature of men would make it impossible to decline the charms of a willing female. She'd been wrong.

Xavier was every bit as passionate as she might have hoped, but a thousand times more discriminating. He wasn't holding her simply because she was there. He was holding her because he wished to. Because they *both* wished to. And oh, did she love his kisses.

His hand cradled the back of her head as his mouth claimed hers. She slid her fingers into his hair, reveling in the sensation. Her pulse raced.

She could scarcely credit that the moment was even happening. Each kiss, each touch, imprinted onto her brain. Every inch of her body felt electric and alive. It was even better than she'd imagined.

This was Xavier's body pressed against hers. His wicked mouth, his teasing tongue, his hair curling about her fingertips. For the moment, he was hers. She would take it. *This* was how it felt to be desired. The moment might not happen again.

When the back of his knuckles brushed against the curve of her bosom, her nipples tightened beneath her shift. Yearning coursed through her like lightning. Her breasts felt fuller.

As his fingertips skated slowly across one of the taut peaks, a wave of arousal flooded her. Her legs trembled. He was more than she'd hoped, and everything that she'd ever wanted. She prayed he'd never stop.

Breathless, she arched into his touch. His hand cupped her breast as his fingers teased her nipple. Her breath stuttered. She had never felt so pretty, so powerful. No wonder courtesans held themselves like queens. She felt invincible.

He lowered his head to her bodice. When his mouth closed around her nipple, she gasped as a shiver of ecstasy radiated through her. This was what she'd been waiting for. She gripped his hair, clutching him to her—

And screamed as claws raked down her spine.

Xavier sprang backward, panting, his eyes wide with surprise. "Did I hurt you?"

"It's not you," she gritted out, wincing at the weight of the cat tangled in her hair and cleaving to her skin. Gingerly, she turned her back toward the firelight.

"God's teeth. Is that…"

"Yes," she managed through pain-clenched teeth. "Please remove him from me as quickly and carefully as possible."

Xavier leapt forward.

She closed her eyes and concentrated on breathing. The moment the devil cat was disengaged from her spine, she intended to trap the little demon in his wicker cage for the rest of the night. Or the rest of his life.

"Rowr!"

Egui's weight was suddenly gone from her back, but her hair was being torn in a thousand directions at once. She balled her hands into fists. That cat was on his last life. "Once you get him clear, hold on to him while I fetch his basket."

Her hair fell back around her shoulders. Xavier stepped away. *"Hurry."*

She ran.

She careened into the bedchamber and scooped up the basket without slowing. Within seconds, she was back in the parlor. She slammed the lid closed the moment Xavier dumped Egui inside and quickly fastened the double latch. There. She seized the howling, rattling basket and tried to catch her breath.

"Turn around." Xavier's voice was stiff. The magic was gone. "I need to see your wounds."

She set down the basket and slowly turned around.

One by one, the buttons of her gown popped free. Her shoulders slumped. A few minutes ago, he might've undressed her for far better reasons than playing nurse. It was over. They would never share a moment like that again.

Her hands flew to her chest as her dress gaped forward. Cool air trickled down her back. He was already loosening her stays. She held as still as she could. He tugged down the thin linen of her shift to expose her back.

"You've got several long scratches, but no blood." He straightened her shift and shoved his thumbs into his waistband. "Good night, Miss Downing. I'm going to try and get some sleep. Although I doubt that I'll have much of that while you're here."

"Jane," she whispered, clutching her loose gown to her chest.

He inclined his head. "Good night, Jane."

He held her gaze for an extra beat, then turned and walked away.

Shoulders sagging, she left Egui in his basket in the parlor and trudged back to the bedchamber. He was right. It would be a long night.

After changing into her night-rail, she was still far too tense to sleep. She retrieved a novel from her luggage and settled the stool closer to the firelight.

No matter how many times she read the lines on the page, she failed to comprehend a single word. She couldn't stop thinking about Xavier. He could've slept with her, right here in this bed.

He *should've* slept with her.

His insistence on clinging to proper sleeping arrangements was honorable and admirable and could not help but raise her esteem... but this was his house. This was his bed. He should be in it.

At last, she tossed the book aside. Reading was impossible. So was sleep. She would check on Egui and look in on Xavier, and perhaps then she might be able to get some rest.

She lit a taper in the fireplace and slipped out into the hall.

The parlor was dark. Few embers remained behind the grate. She inched forward. Egui's basket was still where she left it. The latch was in place. The beast wasn't howling. She didn't suppose she could ask for much more.

After a moment's hesitation, she continued on to the servants' quarters. If the door was closed, she would not knock. Xavier deserved his sleep.

But if he were awake, and desirous of conversation...

She paused three paces from the door. It was ajar, but no light flickered within. She shivered at the sudden chill.

This side of the cottage was freezing. She frowned at the darkness on the other side of the door. Was there no fire in the hearth? She nudged the door open a crack. The room was pitch-black and ice-cold. Her teeth chattered at the marked change in temperature.

Xavier lay on his side in a thin, narrow bed. Even from this distance, she could see him trembling.

Realization hit her. The daft man would rather freeze to death than share their body heat. Well, she didn't have to agree.

She crept forward. There was no way a man this stubbornly honorable could be talked into retaking his bedchamber. Yet she couldn't let him freeze. She blew out her candle and climbed in next to him.

Almost immediately, she realized he wasn't trembling because of the cold, but rather suffering from a bad dream. His muscles twitched alarmingly. Little gasps escaped his throat at uneven intervals.

"Shh. It's all right. I'm here now." She touched a tentative hand to his shoulder.

He flew out of the bed, his fists held up high. "What? What?"

She swallowed, nervous. "It's me. I just—"

"Jane?" His voice lost all vestiges of sleep. "What the devil are you doing in here?"

"It was cold and I thought you needed... body heat?" she stammered. Her face was burning. In the darkness, she couldn't make out his features. She wished she hadn't blown out the candle.

"Body heat." His voice was skeptical. And much closer than she'd calculated. In the space of a breath, he scooped her into his arms and carried her down the hall. "You're not sleeping in there, Jane. There's no fire."

When they reached his bedchamber, she half expected him to toss her onto the mattress and walk away.

He did not. To her surprise, he placed her gently in the center and then lay down beside her. He covered them both with a blanket.

"Go to sleep," he ordered her gruffly, hauling her into his embrace. "I won't let you catch cold."

Warmth spread through her as she snuggled into him. This was what she had wanted.

Perhaps they could be there for each other.

Chapter Thirteen

JANE WAS DISAPPOINTED when she woke up alone.

She was delighted, however, when Xavier re-appeared in the bedchamber a few moments later with two large buckets of steaming water.

"Is this when we strip naked?" she asked with a salacious smile.

He opened the curtains to his dressing closet to reveal a beautiful bathing tub. "This is when *you* do, saucy wench. I'll have my chance later. I've got more snow melting in the kitchen."

She pushed back the covers and swung her feet out of bed. "If we're not bathing each other, why are you in such high spirits?"

He paused on his way toward the door to glance back at her over his shoulder. "The snow has finally stopped."

A chill wracked through her that had nothing to do with the cold. Their magical interlude was over. And he was *pleased*.

She wrapped her arms around her chest and tried not to show her dejection. "I suppose I'm off, then? After breakfast?"

"More likely after tomorrow's breakfast. The snowstorm has ended, but the roads are impassable. I doubt we'll see any traffic today." He smiled at her. "But take heart. The sooner you return home, the less likely anyone will know that you were ever here."

Her return smile was brittle. She half expected him to pat her on the head and tell her to wash behind her ears like a good girl. She didn't *want* to go home. Not yet. He thought the best thing for both of them would be for her to walk away.

She was going to have to change his mind.

When he quit the room, she hurried out of bed and into the bath before it cooled. She sighed with pleasure as she sank into the tub. The luxury of hot water was exactly what she needed.

Now, if only she could get what she *wanted:* Captain Xavier Grey.

She bit her lip. Years ago, her interest in him had been limited to his dark good looks. He was something pretty to look at, but she hadn't given much more thought than that. No one had. Until that dashing but untitled young man had set off to become an even more dashing war hero. If he'd been a romantic figure before, he became positively irresistible. Every female in London whispered his name. *Have you seen that handsome Captain Grey? Even without regimentals, he's a sight to behold. If he pierced* me *with those captivating blue eyes, I'd swoon on the spot.*

Jane stared down at the water. Like the others, she had been entranced by the romance and excitement of the presence of a real hero. When she'd drawn up her list of men with whom she'd be willing to have a liaison, his had been the only name on it. Her body had never been in any doubt about who to choose.

But during their days snowbound together, something changed.

As she got to know him, she began to want him with her brain just as much as her body. He read books. He cooked her meals. He brushed her hair. He was *nice*. He protected her from the cold and from herself. He let her ask questions he didn't wish to answer. He saw her for who she truly was... and still liked her. He'd asked her to dance. He wasn't a hero, but a *person*. With needs and regrets and dreams just as powerful as hers.

She hadn't let herself believe in love because she was certain men didn't believe in the emotion, either. She'd been wrong. Xavier cared about forever, not easy conquests. He'd made her realize she should, too. That it was a mistake to agree to anything less. She was no longer certain she even could.

Being his lover—or even his mistress—was no longer feasible. She couldn't settle for a few nights. Not when she wanted him for much, much longer. Her stomach twisted.

In order to have any chance, she was going to have to prove to him that *he* was lovable. That he deserved forever, too.

Continued attempts at seduction wouldn't sway him. Arguments wouldn't help. She was down to her last gambit: She would simply have to be Jane. And show him that being himself was more than enough.

He didn't have to walk on glass. He was worthy exactly as he was. She *wanted* him exactly as he was.

With a smile, she quit the tub and began to dry her body and her hair. She and Xavier were made for each other. He wished to divorce himself from High Society? She wouldn't oppose him.

The only reason she attended routs at all was because those circles were the closest she came to having friends. Even if she'd never quite fit, those outings were something to do, somewhere to be.

She'd had no other choice. Until now.

With Xavier, they could make their own society. Free from pressure to conform to what the *beau monde* expected a bluestocking or a soldier to be. They didn't need the *ton*. They would have their friends, and each other. What else mattered?

If he became her suitor, he would find himself courting a strong-willed young lady who was as sensual as any woman and as daring as any man.

She would simply have to show him how much fun that could be.

Xavier was already perfect for her. He patently wished for her to be happy. His preoccupation with returning her home with her reputation intact was for her benefit, not his.

When was the last time someone had done something exclusively for her benefit? What better proof could there be that this once-lost hero was the one man with whom she should share her life? She just had to prove it to him, too.

Now, before it was too late.

As soon as she was dressed—save for tightening her stays and fastening the row of buttons up her spine—she opened the bedchamber door and peeked out into the hall.

Egui's basket had changed position. Xavier must have already taken him outside. Perhaps that was when he'd realized the snow had ceased.

Anxiety flooded her at the thought of the melting snow. This was her last chance. She twisted her fingers. How could she shake him out of his closed mindset in just one night?

Xavier stepped around the corner looking windblown and devastatingly handsome. He smiled when he saw her.

She hurried forward to meet him. "Did you just come in from outside?"

"You wouldn't believe how cold it is out there." He gave an exaggerated shudder. "Then again, nothing can compare with the freezing temperatures in Belgium."

This was it. Her heart pounded. "I'll take that bet."

"What bet?" His forehead creased, then cleared. He shook his head. "You want to wager on which winters were the worst? You'll lose. I was in the army for three years. You've never experienced a Belgian winter. Despite the past few days, it's always better in Mother England."

"What do I get if I win?" she insisted.

He turned her around to begin lacing her stays. "How about this. If you win, you get to plan the day's activities. If I win, there *are* no activities. You stay in the cottage. I shovel."

Perfect. "I win."

"How do you win?" He burst out laughing. "This is a silly wager. On what grounds can anyone win?"

"On the grounds that it's not colder in Belgium. Mathematically, the historic average March temperatures are one degree warmer in Brussels than in Chelmsford." She couldn't hold back a grin. "I'm afraid Mother England has let you down. Essex is not only colder, but demonstrably more likely to be cloudier, foggier, and windier."

His fingers moved from her stays to her gown. "Demonstrably how?"

"Almanacs," she answered cheerfully. "You've the same ones in your library, if you don't believe my numbers. And before you say they're three years old, I kept up with more recent figures via newspapers. The pattern holds."

"England has certainly changed while I've been away." His voice was droll. "Bluestockings memorize historic climate data on every major city in Europe now?"

"Not every city. I've no idea what winters are like in Prague or Rome. I only looked up places I knew you'd fought in or lived in." She bit her lip. "I wasn't trying to learn weather patterns. I was trying to get to know *you*."

He finished buttoning her gown in silence, then turned her to face him. His eyes were unfathomable. "When did you do this?"

"Study Belgium? When you and the others returned from war." Her cheeks burned. "I learned of your home in Chelmsford more recently. That's why the slight discrepancy was fresh in my mind."

His gaze was soft as he brushed the pad of his thumb across her cheekbone and cupped the side of her face. "All right. You win. What are our plans for the day?"

Chapter Fourteen

A TENDRIL of sweet-smelling smoke curled up from the cheroot clutched between her teeth as Xavier's ever-surprising houseguest slapped triple aces onto the table and reached for the pile of betting fish.

Again.

He didn't know what was worse—that his nightmare of contributing to a proper young lady's descent into total debauchery was playing out in lurid color, or that he was secretly enjoying the constant upheaval of having Jane in his life. She knew scotch from whiskey, had no trouble counting markers, and almost certainly dealt her cards from the bottom of the deck.

She was absolutely shameless.

He hadn't had this much fun in years.

More precisely, he hadn't had *fun* in years. He tossed down his own trio of aces and scooped the chips right out of Jane's hands. Between war and shutting himself off from society upon his return, he'd quite forgotten how delightful an evening of poor sportsmanship and raucous laughter could be.

He'd never expected to relive that feeling again, much less here, tonight. With her.

Her lush mouth fell open when she saw his cards. "You can't have three aces!"

"Why not?" He gave her an innocent gaze as he raked in his winnings. "You do."

She spluttered, then collapsed into laughter. "I thought I was the only one with a spare deck. Two of yours are the ace of spades!"

"Never underestimate a soldier," he warned her gravely. "We always carry spades."

She threw a handful of cards at him. "I'll give you an extra one, right through the heart."

"You wound me, madam." He pushed all the cards to the far side of the table and shook a new set from a fresh deck. "Double stakes?"

"Hmm." She twirled her glass of port. "All or nothing?"

"You're on." He began to deal.

Her hair was loose about her shoulders. She'd lost the pins right about the time he'd poured her port. The long, soft chestnut waves fell down her back and caressed every curve. It took all of his strength not to shove his fingers into that beautiful hair and kiss her until he drowned.

She had enchanted him. It was impossible to keep fighting it. Over the past few days, he had slowly realized that although Jane was a wallflower and a bluestocking and a virgin, she wasn't *just* those things.

Anyone this diverting didn't have to be a wallflower. She'd already admitted to being a bluestocking by choice. And her presence on his doorstep hadn't been by accident.

Everything she did, she did because she wished to. If she was here with him, it was because she meant to be.

He felt oddly proud at having been the one to catch her attention. She made him feel like he was the only man who mattered. "I find it hard to believe that you don't have a dozen beaux at any one time."

She wiggled her eyebrows. "Because of the seductive way I light a cigar?"

"That," he admitted with a rakish grin, "and everything else. You're smart, you're beautiful, and you cheat at cards. Why aren't you married?"

The easy laughter faded from her eyes. She stubbed out her cheroot in its dish. "You mean, why don't I throw myself on the tender mercies of the Marriage Mart? You're right. Isaac could find *someone* interested enough in me or my dowry to make the march to the altar. But I refuse to marry someone I don't want. Why should I?"

"Lots of people do."

"I won't. Never again." She reached for her cards. "Losing my fiancé was the best thing that ever happened to me."

"Your *what?*" A white-hot streak of jealousy ripped through him. He forced his tone to modulate. "You were to wed? What happened?"

She picked through her cards without meeting his eyes. "It didn't work out."

"How in the world did being betrothed not work out?"

"Many ways." She rubbed her temple. "Besides, it's in the past."

He narrowed his eyes at the evasion. "How far in the past?"

Her gaze slid away. She set down her cards and began sorting her markers. "I was almost seventeen. It would've been a small wedding."

His stomach twisted. "A bride at *sixteen?* How old was he?"

"Five-and-thirty. It didn't happen. Don't look so thunderous. Isaac agreed I was too young for suitors and talked our guardian into letting me wait a few years. As soon as Isaac gained his majority, he got a town house and brought me to London to make my curtsey."

His hands clenched and unclenched. "What happened to your ex-intended?"

She shrugged. "He was someone else's suitor by then. Besides, *I* never intended to have him. That decision was made for me. My guardian didn't want wards."

Fury gnawed at him. A sixteen-year-old girl had no business being wed against her will. "Who is this paragon that wanted a young girl for his bride? And who the devil was your guardian at the time?"

"It doesn't matter." She pushed away her stacks of betting fish and shrugged. "That was then. I was young."

"That's exactly why it matters!"

"That's exactly why it doesn't. Eight years change a person. Besides, he probably doesn't remember my name."

"I wish I knew *his*." Xavier cracked his knuckles.

"Why? He's irrelevant. I haven't seen him in years." Her voice grew softer. "I stayed in the shadows for a long time, and by the time I wanted out, it was too late. I was invisible. No one noticed me, no matter how hard I tried. For years, I blamed everyone else. And then I thought—why *not* go after what I want?" She smiled up at him from beneath her lashes. "What I wanted was you. That's why I'm here. No matter what happens, I won't regret it. I got to know the man you really are."

He stared back at her in consternation. If only her words were true. If only it were *possible* to know what kind of man he really was and not regret it. He shoved his fingers through his hair. He liked her, too. Despite himself. It had been easier to push her away, easier to say no, when all they'd shared was physical attraction.

Of course he desired her. That long, magnificent hair. The curve of her arse. The swell of her breasts. Her plump pout. Those incredible brown eyes. He longed to watch them darken with passion as she locked her legs around his hips and made love to him.

Except then there'd be an *after*. She deserved so much more than any of the afters he could give. He couldn't marry her. Wouldn't wish anyone the bad fortune to be leg-shackled to him for eternity. He was not a good man. He'd make a terrible husband.

Which left what? Giving in to her desire to be his lover? She didn't deserve that either, no matter how much he wanted her. She deserved a man who would never let her walk away.

He picked up his cards and tried to focus. The suits blurred. Concentration was impossible. All he could think about was her.

From the moment she'd walked in his front door, it had just been a matter of time. And willpower. With every saucy little grin, every surprise, every ace up her sleeve, she dug herself a little deeper into his heart. He *cared* about her.

All the more reason to keep her safe, not seduced.

He drained his whiskey. No matter what she thought about the prospects for her future, she would make some other man a wonderful wife. In fact, he couldn't imagine a better partner.

At first, he'd assumed a woman like Jane Downing would be the last person he'd be able to talk to or relate to. He'd been wrong. Her very bluestockingness meant she was the only non-soldier of his acquaintance that was familiar with the geography of Belgium, who kept up with the war and its soldiers beyond the sightings of officer regimentals in the scandal sheets.

More than that, she knew her history. Not just Napoleon, but any major war, going back for centuries. She could put things into context in ways he'd never even considered.

All this, without having lost her innocence. She might think her books made her world weary, but her lack of personal experience with life's horrors kept her innocent. She believed in the causes all those people died for. She believed in *him*.

It was almost enough to make him feel like it was possible. Like he could become a good person again, if he tried hard enough and wanted it bad enough.

The first step would be doing the right thing by Miss Downing.

Which meant as much as he liked her, as much as he ached to give in to desire and pull her close, the best thing he could do for them both was to keep his distance. Even if he had to drink himself into a stupor just to keep from touching her.

He gestured toward the table with his glass of whiskey. "Your move, milady."

Before either of them could play the first card, an ear-piercing screech filled the air. A gray blur flew across the table, sending cards and markers spraying into the air like so much confetti.

"Get him!" Jane leaped up and fled the room.

No problem. He was an ex-soldier.

He set down his whiskey. As he lurched to his feet, his chair tumbled over backward and clattered to the floor. The cat jerked its head toward the sudden noise, which gave Xavier just enough time to launch himself atop and trap Egui in his arms.

The cat thanked him with a full set of claws.

Jane raced back into the room with the wicker basket she used as a cage. "We'll need some new string. He chewed through the latch."

"Hard to imagine," Xavier gritted out whilst attempting to keep the beast immobile. "I hate to say it, but your cat is a menace."

She knelt before him and opened the basket. "Egui isn't my cat."

He paused and tried to focus. "What?"

"Egui." She positioned the basket like a box trap. "He's not my cat. If I had a cat, it would be well behaved. And I'd name him something more sensible. Perhaps... Ambrose. Or Mr. Whiskers."

Xavier shifted to one side. "What kind of name *is* Egui?"

"A Chinese one. It means 'hungry ghost.' That's why he can't resist eating linen." She motioned for him to release the cat. "Gently. My

brother will cry if anything happens to his pre-
cious fur demon."

The cat shot out of his hold and straight into
the basket. It was certainly as hard to catch as a
ghost. And it spared no linens.

Xavier sat up and rubbed his new welts. "I
don't always know when you're teasing."

"I'm never teasing." She tied down the basket
lid with a ribbon of cloth that looked suspiciously
like the lining of his new waistcoat.

"Do you and your brother speak Chinese?"

She finished tying the knot. "I do not."

He blinked. "Then how did this cat get that
kind of a name?"

"We don't know. He already had that moni-
ker when he came to us. Isaac is watching him
for a friend."

"A Chinese friend?" he guessed, feeling lost.

"Obviously." She tested the knot's hold.
"How else would Egui get a Chinese name?"

"How did your brother get a Chinese *friend?*"
Who was this family? Xavier felt like he was living in an Italian farce. Any minute now, dancers
would burst onstage and put the whole situation
to music. He was almost disappointed that they'd
missed their cue.

Jane pushed the basket into the furthest corner of the room. "How would I know? I didn't
know Isaac had any friends until Egui showed up
and demanded his rightful place as supreme ruler
of our household."

"How long ago was that?"

She pursed her lips thoughtfully. "Nine years."

His jaw fell open. Nine years. They'd been looking after a devil-possessed feline for nine long years. Just the thought made his skin tingle with dread.

He shook his head. "I'm afraid your brother doesn't have a Chinese friend. He has a very clever Chinese enemy."

"You're bleeding." She lifted his hands to inspect his shredded sleeves. "Come with me. I have a special salve in my valise."

Of course she did. She was the keeper of a hungry cat demon.

And yet, it didn't detract from her charms. If anything, it made her all the more surprising and mysterious. He could spend every moment of the rest of his life with this woman and never have a single boring day.

Or a single boring night. There was no better distraction from the scratches on his arms than the sway of her hips as she walked. All he had now was the familiar ache in his heart at the thought of her leaving.

This would be their last evening together.

As soon as they entered the bedchamber, she stripped him of his coat. His waistcoat. His shirt-sleeves.

He'd foregone a cravat this morning because he couldn't find any non-shredded ones. Now he wished he'd worn ten shirts, just to feel her fingers unbuttoning him, again and again.

Cool air met hot skin. His chest was naked, his arms bare.

She wasn't looking at him like a field nurse inspecting a soldier for wounds. The catch in her throat and the jump in her pulse indicated she saw him for what he was. A man.

A half-naked one.

She held one of his forearms above the basin of water. He let her. She lifted a sponge from the basin with a trembling hand and daubed it gently along his arm.

He didn't care about the scrapes. He couldn't tear his eyes from hers. The dark curve of her eyelashes against the pale white of her cheeks. The way she nibbled her rosy lower lip. The sweet smell of her hair. How he yearned to take her in his arms and show her how much she meant to him.

She reached for his other wrist. "Almost done. Then I'll get the salve."

"I don't need salve." His voice was husky and raw.

Her lips parted. She gazed up at him, eyes wide. "What do you need?"

"You."

Chapter Fifteen

THE SPONGE FELL from Jane's hand, forgotten.

Yes. A thrill shot through her as Xavier's mouth covered hers. At last, she could do with her fingers as she pleased. She splayed them against his bare chest and shivered at the feel of her naked palms against his hot male flesh.

She ran her hands up over his shoulders and clasped them about his neck. His warmth seeped through her clothes, heating her skin. An entire library of erotic sketches wouldn't have prepared her for so many conflicting sensations.

Her stays were suddenly too tight, her shift suffocating. But all she could do was press even closer and lose herself in his kisses.

His lips against hers were firm, insistent. Her heart thudded. He wasn't the only one who wanted more. She wanted everything. She wanted *him*. Her lips parted, demanding.

He swept his tongue into her mouth to toy with hers. Every touch was a teasing promise of what it might do, how it would feel, upon the rest of her body. Her breath came faster. She hadn't forgotten the joy of his tongue against her breast. She longed for it.

His body was strong and hard beneath her fingertips, yet the hair at the nape of his neck was soft and silky. Desire began to coil deep within her. She wanted to explore the rest of his body. She wanted him to explore hers.

Her secret book of sketches was nothing compared to this. A mere hint of future pleasure. Some illustrations had depicted a man placing his open mouth upon his lover's breast or betwixt her thighs. But the drawings had failed to show how dizzying it felt to have his open mouth on hers, to quake with delicious anticipation.

One of his hands traveled slowly down her spine to the small of her back. She held her breath, hoping he would loosen the buttons as he went. Her tongue became just as demanding as his.

"Feel me, Jane," he murmured against her mouth. "I want you."

He grabbed her hips and hauled her to him. The proof of his arousal was now flush against her belly, every inch as hot and hard as he was. He desired *her*. A bolt of power raced through her. Nothing could be more erotic.

He slid his palm up her rib cage to the curve of her breast. Her nipples instantly hardened. She moaned as his fingers teased one at a time. The thin layers of her gown were too much of a barrier.

"Unbutton me," she begged. "Please."

His mouth covered hers, claiming her. He tasted of whiskey and wicked promise. She sank her fingers into his hair and arched into him. He smiled against her lips, then deepened the kiss. One by one, the buttons along her spine popped free. She held her breath.

At last, her dress fell forward. She pushed her arms through the sleeves and let the gown tumble to the floor. Only her shift remained. She reached behind her back to loosen the stays.

He stilled her hand, his eyelids heavy with passion. "I'm in no hurry."

"*I* am." She peered up at him from beneath her lashes. This was her chance to finally have him in her arms. To experience passion with someone who cared about her. "I want to feel my body against yours."

He turned her around. "As you wish."

She twisted her hair in one hand and held it above her head to afford him easier access. Cool air kissed the back of her neck, but only for a second.

As he unlaced her stays, he pressed open-mouthed kisses to her neck and shoulders. Each kiss reverberated through her body, stealing her breath. Once she was freed, he cast her stays aside. His lips were dark with desire when he spun her back to face him.

"I can't fight it anymore," he rasped, pulling her close. "Yes or no?"

There was no mistaking his intention. Or hers.

"Yes." She had never been more certain. At last he would be hers, even if for just one night. She would simply make the most of it.

She lifted her shift over her head and flung it next to her stays. Her slippers were next. Now nothing covered her, save the silk stockings gartered just above her knees. She was naked before him. Yet she'd never felt so beautiful.

He drank her in as if her body filled him with wonder. The rise and fall of his chest indicated his heart sped just as fast as hers. Without another word, he scooped her into his arms and carried her to the bed.

She reached for him as her head fell back onto the pillow. He immediately discarded his boots and lay down beside her.

"Your breeches?" she prompted.

"Not yet." He cupped the side of her face and slanted his mouth over hers.

She reveled in the heat of his mouth and the chill of her bare skin in the cool air. The hearth warmed her feet and cast a soft glow about the chamber, but the only warmth she craved was the heat of his body. Her entire body tingled.

Without breaking their kiss, he splayed his hand just below her bosom. Her breast swelled in anticipation of his touch.

When at last he cupped her flesh, she sighed with pleasure. His fingers pinched and teased her nipples until she arched toward him, panting. Surely he could feel the thrum of her heart through the palm of his hand.

He lifted his lips from hers only to lower his head and take one of her sensitive nipples into his mouth. She moaned. His hand slid down over her stomach until it covered the juncture of her thighs. He glanced up from her breast, as if asking permission.

She spread her legs, allowing him access. It wasn't permission. It was a demand.

The illustrations she'd seen indicated a man could work as much magic with his fingers as with his member. She had every intention of finding out.

Just as he turned his mouth to her other breast, he slid his fingertips between her legs. Pleasure shot through her. She felt swollen and needy. This was heaven. She grabbed his hair as his wet fingers brought her close to the edge.

He slid from her grasp and lowered his mouth to join his hand. Her eyes fluttered backward in rapture as his tongue and fingers emulated what she hoped their bodies would soon do in earnest.

"Breeches," she croaked, gripping the blanket in fistfuls. *"Off."*

He ignored her. His fingers and tongue continued his slow, steady assault on her senses. The pressure that had been building within her grew to a crescendo. She threw her head back. Her legs stiffened about his shoulders as waves of pleasure burst from within.

Only when she fell limp atop the blanket did he leap to his feet and shuck his breeches before returning to the bed.

He held her cheek and kissed her as he eased his member between her legs. She was slick and ready from her recent release, but still he could only enter her a fraction of an inch at a time. Pain shot through her.

He froze. "I'm hurting you."

"I wanted you to." Already the pain was receding. She reveled in the feel of him within her. This was not *her* moment. It was *their* moment. She licked his lower lip. "I want you. *All* of you."

"Thank God." He slanted his mouth over hers.

Gently, deliberately, he began to move within her. The pleasure began to build. She had never felt such utter abandon. His breath was as uneven as her own. When at last he was sheathed fully within her, she gasped into his mouth and wrapped her legs tightly about him.

His kisses became hotter as his thrusts grew deeper. Lovemaking was everything she'd ever longed for, and more. The sweet pressure between her legs coiled once more and her hips rose to meet him. She panted and pulled him close. The friction was dizzying. She couldn't possibly give this up. Or him. They were too perfect. He made her feel… He made her *feel*.

He fixed his blue eyes on her mouth. Tremors rocked her legs and she held on tight. She reached her climax with their gazes locked together. If it had been incredible with his fingers, she was struck wordless by the sensation of him driving within her as her muscles contracted around him.

His hips bucked. He jerked free and grunted as he spilled his seed into the blanket. Without raising his head, he flung a heavy arm about her and pulled her close.

She curled against him and pressed a kiss to his bare skin. He tasted faintly salty. The entire room was spiced with their lovemaking. She felt like she belonged. Like she could stay in this bed with him forever.

He cuddled her close. His eyes drifted shut as she laid her cheek against him. Peace enveloped her. This was everything she hadn't known she wanted. She felt cherished. And finally happy.

Xavier stroked her hair until his breathing slowed to a calm, steady pace. She threaded her fingers in his dark, silky hair. He had fallen asleep.With a smile, she snuggled closer.

She was almost asleep when Xavier's heartbeat quickened. Her eyes flew open. His breaths became shallow and irregular. She propped herself up in alarm. His muscles twitched as if he were struggling against invisible bonds.

She touched her fingertips to his shoulder. "Xavier?"

He shot upright, his eyes wide and unseeing. Sweat matted his hair to his scalp. His breath was uneven.

She pulled her hands back. "I didn't mean to wake you. When I realized you were having another nightmare, I…"

His head slowly turned toward hers. His face was ashen, but his gaze was cold and dark. He picked her hand up off his thigh and deposited it onto the mattress. "I'm my own nightmare, Miss Downing. I'm the thing in the dark that other people are afraid of."

"Jane," she whispered. "I'm Jane. We just made love." But he wasn't listening. He wasn't even looking at her.

He was shoving his legs into his breeches and reaching for his shirt.

"Where are you going?"

"Out," he grunted.

She hated the querulous tremor in her voice. "Out of doors?"

"Out of this bedchamber. Any other questions?"

Her heart twisted. "You don't have to be ashamed of nightmares. Many soldiers who return from battle find that it takes time to assimilate into their old lives. I know war is terrible, but you can take heart in the fact that—"

"Can I, Jane?" he mocked.

Her stomach sank. She'd somehow made things worse. "I just meant—"

"War is terrible?" His laugh was ugly. "You don't know the first thing about it."

"I know you," she said staunchly. At least, she thought she did.

He snorted. "You know what you want me to be, so that's all you see. I've told you repeatedly that I'm no hero. I didn't even return from *battle*. I haven't fired a musket in two years."

She shook her head in confusion. "You weren't in battle?"

"There's more to an army than soldiers." His eyes were dark, his mouth twisted. "I wasn't anywhere near Waterloo. The *beau monde* romanticizes the military until anyone in uniform is a demigod in their own right. They're fools."

"I wouldn't say it's been... romanticized..." She trailed off. He was right. Obviously it had. "You're still a hero. I meant it when I said that fighting for your country is inherently good, even if you have to do bad things."

"I used to think that, too. Now I can't sleep at night." His eyes were dark, his face pale. The cords stood out on his neck. "Everyone fought for their country. Not everyone did what I did. They're calling my friends and me the 'Dukes of War' as if we've done a noble, heroic thing. Perhaps the others did, but I did not. I don't deserve accolades or some romantic appellation. I don't deserve to be spoken about at all."

She clutched the blanket to her chest to hide her trembling and her nakedness. "If you weren't in battle, where were you?"

His lips were a dark sneer among the shadows. "You mean, what was I doing that could possibly be worse than shooting men with bullets or running them through with sabers?"

"Yes." Her voice was barely audible above the beating of her heart. "I suppose that is what I meant."

"I helped 'interrogate' captives. Is that heroic? Forcing the enemy to spill their secrets? My commanding officers thought so. I was expected to follow orders, like a good soldier. So I did. The assumption was that any enemy soldier we captured might possess useful information. Sometimes they did."

"And sometimes they didn't?" she whispered.

His face was hard. "Sometimes they died."

She scrambled backward in shock. He was right. He wasn't the man she thought he was. He *was* the thing in the dark that other people were afraid of. Or at least, he had been.

Could she accept him for the man he was now?

Chapter Sixteen

XAVIER HAD THOUGHT disillusionment would
be the worst thing he could bring to Jane's face.
He was wrong.

There was no point in saying, *I'm not going
to hurt you.* He'd taken her virginity with one
thrust, and now he was destroying whatever was
left of her innocence.

He swallowed against the sour taste in the
back of his mouth. It was time she knew the truth.
He would *never* be the man she imagined him to
be. He had lost that hope years ago.

But he hated to see her hunched against the
headboard of the bed they'd just shared, clutching the blankets to her naked breasts and staring
at the foot of the bed with... disappointment?

Perhaps she wasn't *afraid* of him. She simply
regretted she'd ever met him.

He hadn't meant things to go this far. The
days with her were so damn exhilarating, and he
wasn't made of steel. He was made of broken
promises.

Xavier shoved his shaking fingers into his hair and looked away as self-recrimination washed through him. He'd wanted her to understand. But not like this. Not now.

At last she comprehended the imprudence of offering her body to an illusion she'd constructed in her mind. And he hadn't stopped her. He'd *known* it was wrong, and he'd done nothing to prevent the natural conclusion from playing out.

He hadn't changed at all.

Perhaps he couldn't. Perhaps he was doomed to make the same mistakes for the rest of his ill-conceived life.

"What did you do?" she whispered. Her eyes did not meet his. "Start at the beginning."

He almost laughed. The beginning. When was that? He'd been born the year the French Revolution began. No one romanticized battle better than a young boy. He couldn't aspire to riches or inheriting a title, but could absolutely join the King's Army and earn the admiration and respect of all.

Nothing ever went according to plan.

"I purchased my commission with my closest friends," he said at last. "But we were separated after training. I found myself surrounded by strangers. All of them young, all of them scared, and all of them willing to die rather than be seen as less of a soldier than their compatriots." His throat grew thick. "I fit in perfectly."

Silence stretched through the chamber.

When Jane again spoke, her voice was hesitant. "This is why you said that not everything one does for one's country is good after all?"

"I understand why you believe that. I did, too. We all did." He could hear the bitterness in his voice. And the repressed anger. "I gave everything I had to everything I did, and was rewarded handsomely for it." His mouth twisted. "But it wasn't until I was assigned to help oversee the 'questioning' of prisoners that I realized how deceptive our beliefs had become. The 'good of our country' now justified any atrocity against our fellow man."

"Overseer." Her face cleared. "You weren't the perpetrator of the crimes."

"Worse. I was a captain." He would never stop hating himself for earning a promotion under such conditions. "I held rank, power, and the keys to unlock every manacle. I never used the latter."

Her expression grew pensive. "Could you have?"

"I didn't think so." He asked himself that question every day. His inability to correct the past gnawed at his soul. "But we always have choices."

"Then why didn't you?" she asked softly.

He closed his eyes. "I believed defeating Napoleon was the greater good. What was the discomfort of one man if the secrets he spilled saved tens of thousands? But there was no way to know which captives might hold the clue to ending the war without interrogating them all." His legs trembled as memories flooded him. "Some of them were simple soldiers, fighting for their country. They didn't deserve to die."

Her expression was guarded. "You held the keys. But you couldn't just walk around unlocking manacles. Not if it might endanger more people."

He nodded. "Had I balked, they would've thought me a spy myself. A traitor. I would've been 'questioned' until my dying breath."

She squared her shoulders. "Then you didn't have a choice."

"That *was* the other choice." He shrugged. "I made the wrong one."

Her eyes flashed. "Martyring yourself would've saved the other captives?"

He shrugged. "It would've made one less monster."

Silence fell.

His skin prickled. He looked away. What was left to say? Some soldiers were heroes. He was not. End of discussion.

"That's a horrible story," came her quiet voice at last.

He nodded. He was a terrible person. The stain on his sheets proved it. He was destroying lives all over again.

"You're right," she continued. "You were following orders, and those awful men could've done the same to you, but it was still despicable to allow torture to be inflicted on another person."

He winced. Those very words careened about his brain a thousand times a day. Awful. Despicable. Torture.

"It's also over." She met his eyes. "And something you deeply regret. As you should. But just because the past will always be there doesn't mean you can't make the most of your future."

His laugh was harsh and ugly. Just like the man he knew himself to be. "What future do you suggest? Puppies and babies? Shall I call the banns?" He spread his arms wide. "In three short weeks, all this could be yours."

"I wasn't suggesting marriage," she snapped.

Of course she wasn't. No sane woman would.

He lifted a shoulder. "At least you got the meaningless affair you'd wanted."

Her back pressed higher against the wall. "What I *wanted* was to make love with someone I liked, and who liked me. I wanted to feel… like a woman. To connect with another person."

"Well, I'm a man, and men copulate because we have cocks." He knew he was being cruel. She deserved *anyone* but him. He needed to ensure she ran back to safety and never returned. "Men like me don't connect, Miss Downing. We think with our ballocks, not our brains."

Her lip trembled. "Or hearts?"

"I don't possess one." He turned his back to the bed. "Get some sleep. You've a long trip ahead of you tomorrow."

Chapter Seventeen

SHE MIGHT NEVER sleep again.

Jane lay in the center of the still-warm bed she'd shared with Xavier just moments before and stretched out her arms in despondency.

How had something so perfect turned out so wrong? She'd meant what she'd said about one's past not determining one's future. But he was right. He wasn't the man she'd thought he was. Possibly not even a man she wanted.

She stared up at the canopy. Perhaps he was right to believe one couldn't escape one's past. Or at least one's past decisions. The faint soreness between her legs loudly proclaimed her own folly.

He'd warned her, time and again. That she couldn't change her mind and recover her virginity. That the loss of her maidenhead was permanent. That he was the wrong man to give it to. She gulped. Too late now. She could never undo those choices.

A chill swept across her skin. The past might not fully determine the future, but she now saw how one's actions might stick with you.

His experiences under the umbrella of war had been horrific. They'd turned him into someone he didn't like, or even recognize.

She couldn't let the same thing happen to her, just because she no longer had her virginity.

But what did that mean? Her fingers grew cold. She'd never really thought about the future. She'd wished for love and friends and passion, but she'd wished to have them *right now*, without considering where she might be five years from now.

If she'd truly wanted a husband, she could've set about making herself into the sort of woman who would be more likely to attract a suitor. She might've been married off years ago.

But she didn't want to pretend to be someone she was not. She curled her hands into fists and slammed them down against the blankets. It wasn't fair to have to become someone else, just to hold the interest of another person.

She swallowed thickly. Was that what she had done to Xavier?

Before they'd exchanged their first word, she'd already decided what sort of person he was. Romantic, dashing. A hero. She'd painted him with broad, fanciful strokes and never bothered to look at the details.

He hadn't deceived her. She was the one who'd drawn conclusions on no more basis than her own imagination. Her chin slumped.

She'd forced him into the role of someone he'd never claimed to be. What right did she have to be disappointed in him for not living up to a standard she'd imposed on him against his will?

Her chest grew tight as she considered it from his perspective. She'd spent four-and-twenty years hating the people who judged—and dismissed—her for her labels, rather than bother to get to know her as a person.

She was not only a bluestocking. She was also a person. A very headstrong, very foolish, very *ruined* person. She let out a ragged breath.

When she'd focused on Xavier as the object of her desire, perhaps she'd done so more cynically than she'd realized. More selfishly. In order to experience a night of secret passions, she needed a man who fit specific criteria. Handsome enough to arouse her interest. Virile enough to share it. Honorable enough to be trusted with the secret.

She needed the perfect man. So she'd forced him into the part.

But he wasn't a perfect man. No one knew that better than Xavier. What he didn't realize was that he was no longer the man he'd been, the man he'd despised. He didn't need to try to be better. He'd already changed.

The question was... could she?

She'd come to Chelmsford believing herself a wallflower who would never find love. Hoping one night of passion would sustain her during the next forty years of spinsterhood. But why did she have to settle for that? Why couldn't she be a bluestocking *and* a lover *and* a wife?

Insight she could've used weeks ago. Her eyes stung. It was too late. By lying with Captain Grey, she'd thrown away her best chance at landing a proper, Society-approved gentleman... But when had she ever wanted one of those?

She squinted up at the dark canopy and tried to be honest. What was she truly looking for in a man?

She'd wanted handsome. Xavier had that in spades. She'd wanted virile. Last night had proved her fantasies were only the beginning.

She'd also wanted honorable. Her fingers slowly unclenched. Captain Grey was not the pristine, sparkling war hero she'd painted him to be, but did that make him any less honorable? She'd forced herself into his house, his life, and his bed, and *he'd* been the one fighting to keep her honor intact every step of the way. Did that make him less perfect, or more so?

She loved him, she realized dully. She loved him, and it no longer mattered. He had chosen to walk away.

Xavier would never be hers.

She hauled herself to her feet and trudged over to the basin of water. Sun streamed through the cracks between the shutters. The faint crunch of carriage wheels rumbled in the distance. She stumbled at the sound. No more snow. Her limbs were sluggish with a mixture of disappointment and relief.

The adventure was over. Time to go home.

She dressed herself as best she could and got all her belongings stuffed back into her trunk. All she needed was Egui—and a ride to the inn—and she and the cat would be on their way back to London. This was the last she'd see of Captain Grey.

Good. She didn't need another man in her life who didn't want her in his. That's what Egui was for.

New carriage wheels sounded from outside the window, then rolled to a stop. Someone was here!

She flung open the bedchamber door and raced to drag her luggage out of the room before anyone caught her in the master chamber.

Xavier strode into the room and took the trunk from her hands without a word. She followed him out to the corridor, but he edged her back inside.

"Let me at least fasten your stays first," he muttered crossly.

"Yes, Captain Crotchety." She lifted her chin. What did he have to be cross about? He was finally getting his wish. She was going home.

"It's my servants," he said, his voice gruff. "They'll be inside at any moment. Egui's in the parlor. I'll bring your luggage." He finished buttoning her gown and tapped her lightly. "Go."

She made it to the parlor just as two loud, ruddy-faced individuals tumbled through the door. If she had to guess, the housekeeper and a stable boy. Mother and son, by the looks of it, and both equally shocked by her presence.

Their congenial laughter died at once. She squirmed under their frank interest.

Xavier walked around the corner with her trunk, his expression and manner as placid as if he were snowbound with bluestockings once or twice a week. "Please summon the hack driver before he leaves. I have his next fare."

The young boy rushed back out into the cold.

The housekeeper had turned her eyes to her employer, as if by carefully avoiding locking gazes with the unknown woman in their midst, the situation would cease being awkward for all of them.

It wasn't working. Jane was mortified.

The stable boy returned with the driver. "There 'e is, sir."

"Thank you, Timmy." He nodded to both servants. "You are excused. There's tea in the kitchen. We will reconvene in an hour."

At those words, the twosome had no choice but to disappear into the servants' quarters and give their master privacy.

Xavier placed her luggage before the driver and handed him a coin. "Please see the lady safely home—"

"To the Dog & Whistle," she interrupted quickly. "I can find a new hack from there."

"As the lady pleases." He inclined his head to the driver. "To the Dog & Whistle."

"Right away." The driver picked up her trunk and began hauling it out to his hack.

All that was left was Egui and herself.

She picked up the wicker basket and took one last, long look at Xavier. Her voice trembled. "If I thought there was anything between us…"

"There's not." His voice was flat.

She sighed. "I know."

He held open the door. Icy wind rushed in.

"I don't judge you for what you did before." Her chest ached as she looked at him. "I judge you for what you're doing now."

His eyes darkened. "What, pray tell, am I doing now?"

"Absolutely nothing." She stepped out into the cold. "Like you always do."

He caught her arm. "I warned you, Miss Downing. I'm no hero."

She held fast to the basket to keep from reaching for him one last time.

He held himself so still, his body fairly thrummed with intensity. She tried to smile, to pretend it was all right. He dropped her arm as if it had scalded him.

"Safe travels," he said curtly. "I doubt we'll meet again."

Her smile cracked. "Even heroes make mistakes."

He stepped back into his cottage, and the door closed tight behind him.

Chapter Eighteen

THAT NIGHT, Xavier couldn't sleep.

Or the next. Or the night after that. Nothing out of the ordinary for a monster like him, other than a new character having cropped up in his nightmares.

Now, when he stared at the prisoners as the weight of a thousand keys rooted him in place, a soft female voice floated through the darkness.

I don't blame you for that. I blame you for what you're doing now.

What am I doing now?

Absolutely nothing.

He awoke bathed in sweat and spent the rest of the night glaring up at his shadowed canopy, his heart galloping wildly.

The snow was gone. So was Jane.

He wished he had them both back.

Or, at least, her admiration. Her blind faith in him as a genuinely good person. He would never experience that again. He slammed his fist against the bedpost. Destroying her illusions about him had destroyed him, too.

If only he *could* be the man she'd believed him to be. The man he'd always hoped he would become.

A man worth believing in.

He would never be that. With a sneer, he pushed out of bed and stalked over to the window. Although still tightly shuttered, dawn was sneaking through the cracks. The sun relentlessly rose, and so must he. No matter how he felt about it.

He turned toward the basin to splash water on his face. It didn't make him feel better. Nothing had, since Jane left. Everything had only felt worse. His shoulders tightened.

Was she right? Had he changed, just by wishing to?

He would never don regimentals again. Nor would he force anyone to do or say anything against his will. But could he ever atone for the past? Did he prove anything by giving up on his future?

His back slumped against the wall. All he could think about was Jane. How much he missed her. How badly he'd hurt her. No matter how much he'd longed to, they should never have made love.

But wasn't that her decision, too? He hadn't tossed her skirts over her head in a dark alley. She'd journeyed to his door with seduction in mind. They were both to blame.

He gazed over at the empty bed. When he remembered the night they shared, it didn't feel like something to be ashamed of. It felt like something to celebrate. She'd thought so, too. He was almost certain of it.

Where was she now? What would happen to her? There'd been no missives, nor mention of her in the society papers. Perhaps she was back to being a quiet little bluestocking as if no part of their interlude had ever happened. He hoped she had. He hoped she *could*.

She hadn't been interested in marriage, but nor had she exhorted him to keep their affair secret. He would die before betraying her, but she couldn't know that. She simply trusted him.

He paced across the room. Come to think of it, he hadn't asked her to keep his secret, either. He simply trusted her with the darkest parts of his soul.

Why? He hadn't confessed his sins to his best friends. They wouldn't understand. What made her different?

She could certainly keep a secret. To her, past mistakes were irrelevant, except for their impact on what lessons he learned from them. After everything he'd done, then and now… she'd accepted him as he was.

And he'd let her go.

Imbecile. He deserved what he got. He pulled off his nightshirt and stalked over to his closet.

His housekeeper had returned a fresh pile of laundered clothes the night before, but he'd been too tired to put them away and too prickly to let anyone else in the room long enough to help him. He wasn't used to help yet. Wasn't certain he ever could be.

Distracted, he picked up the topmost shirt. His arm was halfway through the sleeve before he noticed bright pink buttons had replaced the previous linen-covered ones. The bucolic row of brightly embroidered butterflies encircling the cuff, however, was impossible to miss.

Jane.

He brought his wrist closer to his face and squinted at her handiwork. His eyes widened in recognition. Not Jane. Egui. This was one of the many shirts Xavier had given up for dead after that damned cat ate all the buttons and sharpened its claws on the sleeves.

Perfectly matched thread sewed those tangled ribbons back into a working sleeve. The butterflies were either there to draw attention away from the surgery—or simply because she could. It was her brother's cat, he remembered belatedly. Perhaps the poor bastard had bunnies and butterflies scampering up all his sleeves.

Just like Xavier.

A quick perusal indicated that not one, not two, but *all* of his undershirts and most of his cravats had been similarly "rescued" from the bin.

He laid them out atop his bed in disbelief. One of his waistcoats was even monogrammed with his initials... as a rainbow menagerie of ducks and squirrels frolicked along the hem.

What on earth was her fascination with woodland creatures? The fall of his best breeches even boasted a chirping robin beside each button.

He burst into helpless laughter. Even when she wasn't there, Jane still managed to surprise him. And to have the last laugh. He selected the worst offender and shoved his arms through the sleeves. Nothing for it. He wouldn't be going to Town, which meant for the next several months, he would be wearing designs better suited for a nursery.

He grinned at his sleeves. Incredible. He wished Jane were there right now so they could laugh together and he could hold her close.

His chest ached. Foolishness. This was reality. He pulled on a pair of breeches and sat to buff his Hessians.

Then again, why bother? There was nowhere to go. No one to stay home with. Just him and his house.

He tied a flowery cravat about his neck and scowled at his reflection in the glass. He looked ridiculous. Jane should absolutely be there to see it.

Zeus, he missed her.

Restless, he strode into his library. It didn't feel half as appealing without a fire burning and

Jane sneaking chapters of *Fanny Hill* at the other
end of the chaise longue. It wasn't the same without her.

His heart was cold. He touched his flint to paper and lit the hearth. Nothing would make him
warm again. He threw himself down onto the
cushions and closed his eyes. It didn't help.

All he could think about was her reciting the
Odyssey, and how she'd forgotten the Trojan
horse because she'd—

God's teeth, there wasn't any part of his
house that didn't make him think of Jane. The
bed where they'd made love. The dining table
where they'd drank and gambled. Even his
cursed nightstand with the basin of water she'd
used to bathe his skin. It was hopeless.

He wished he had memories of her all over
England. She'd said she loved the violin. He
wished he could take her to hear all of her favorite orchestras and arrange private concerts at
home for the two of them. He wanted to spend
every evening brushing out her hair while she
read aloud to him from one of the books in their
library. Even if it was eighteenth-century erotica.

Lord help him. He rubbed his face and stared
at the ceiling. He was *in love* with her. His shoulders tensed as he considered his next move.

Now what?

He sat up and peered over the back of the
chaise longue at all the books they had yet to
read. At the house that could be a home. He was

ashamed of taking her as his lover, but he wasn't ashamed of *her*. The real question was whether she'd give *him* another chance. He shot to his feet.

Their relationship didn't have to be secret. If she was willing, he'd like to make it permanent. To make her his. Forever.

He should never have let her walk away.

Even heroes made mistakes.

His hands went clammy. What could he do about it? He didn't even know where she lived. He could ask Grace or Oliver, but not without providing some sort of explanation.

And then there was Jane's brother to contend with. Xavier could scarcely barge in the front door and demand access to the man's sister. Xavier had no wish to duel with Isaac Downing. The rotter was likely to bring Egui as his second.

He needed to meet her on neutral ground. Talk to her. Beg her. *Find* her. If only he—

The play. She was going to be at the Theatre Royal in less than a sennight. She'd told him so herself. His lungs tightened.

He'd have to be there, too.

Chapter Nineteen

JANE STEPPED OUT of the carriage onto blustery Bow Street and took her brother's arm. They were running late, but at least she wasn't alone.

She ducked her head against the brutal wind and hurried into the Theatre Royal. Grace and her family would already be up in Ravenwood's private box, eagerly awaiting the opening chords of *Cymon*. Jane couldn't cry off.

A part of her wished Xavier could be there. Another part of her dreaded the idea of confronting him face-to-face—and being unable to do more than curtsey and inquire about the weather.

Both were ridiculous worries, of course. He was in Chelmsford, not London. And there he planned to stay.

She held fast to her brother's arm as they strode across the empty lobby. The greatest advantage to arriving late was missing out on the usual crush of fashionable well-wishers, all of whom consistently met her for the first time.

Her throat clogged. She was tired of being nobody. Of being dismissed upon sight and just as quickly forgotten. Why was *she* incapable of forgetting past encounters? Try as she might to forget Xavier, every stolen moment was burned indelibly upon her soul. He would be part of her, forever.

She pressed her lips together in a tight line. There was one definitive advantage to the rampant Janenesia afflicting the *ton*. Any other woman in all of England would have been accosted by friends and neighbors and old finishing school acquaintances every step of the illicit journey.

Not Jane. She had even been forgotten in the back of a hackney carriage during her return journey. She'd fallen asleep, and the driver had simply kept driving. If it weren't for Egui clawing out of his basket, who knew where they might have ended up?

Isaac had returned home a few days later, exhausted from his journey but delighted to see his sister and his cat.

Egui, of course, had been the perfect picture of feline docility. Jane did her best to portray the same image. No mad dashes to Essex here. No forbidden nights in the arms of an ex-soldier. No trampled heart, shattered into a thousand pieces.

Just Jane. Lost in a book. Boring as ever.

She hadn't ventured out of the house since returning home. It wouldn't have been seemly without her brother's chaperonage, but even once he'd returned, she hadn't felt like socializing.

What was the point? None of those men were the one she wanted.

Nothing could compare to the evenings she'd shared with Xavier. Her stomach turned. She'd never realized how deeply it would hurt to love a man who didn't want her.

Isaac slowed as they reached Ravenwood's private box. The usher swept the thick velvet curtains aside and motioned them in to take their seats.

"Hurry," whispered Grace, clapping her gloved hands in excitement. She didn't tear her eyes from the stage. "The orchestra is about to begin."

Jane flashed a weak smile at Lord Carlisle and Grace's mother, then took one of the empty seats. Her limbs were heavy with disappointment. Of course Xavier hadn't come. She'd known it was improbable. She hadn't even really wanted to see him.

So why was her throat dry and her shoulders heavy?

She crossed her arms over her twisting stomach and forced herself to stare at the parting curtain.

The orchestra began just as her brother Isaac slid into place beside her.

Life went on, she told herself. She wasn't alone. She had her stalwart brother. Her best friend. A shared opera box on loan from a duke. Her lot might not be what she wished, but it wasn't *horrid*. Just a fortnight ago, she'd believed her life would be perfect, if only she had the memory of a night of passion to keep her warm.

Well, now she did. And her heart was cold as ice.

She stared dully off the balcony as Cymon and Urganda took the stage. She should at least feign interest in the play. There were worse fates than an evening spent with friends and family. She glanced at her brother. She was grateful to have him beside her. It wasn't his fault she was awash in misery. Isaac loved her. Trusted her. He believed he knew what kind of person she was.

He was wrong, of course. She averted her gaze. Did his false belief in her goodness and purity change who she was? She hated to deceive Isaac above all others, but blurting the truth about her duplicity and fallen state would not benefit either of them. Although, even if Isaac were disappointed in her... he'd love her anyway.

Heat pricked her eyes. Nothing was better or worse than unconditional love.

She froze. How had Xavier felt when he'd confessed his secret? Worse than before? His rejection had stung so badly, she'd been thinking more of herself than of him. She'd responded with logic, not love. Dismissing the depths of his guilt. Deriding him for not standing up for himself, for what they'd shared, for her. Was she right to discount him for his failure to fight to keep her?

Or should she have tried a little harder to stand up for him?

Her heart clenched. *She* knew she loved him. She'd also failed to mention it. Before Xavier could be expected to turn his life upside down, he needed to know she would be there by his side. That she understood who he had been, and accepted him for who he was now.

The power of unconditional love came from the knowledge that one possessed it.

Yet she'd left him without so much as a backward glance.

She rubbed her arms. A rustling went through the audience. She let out a deep breath and tried to focus on the play.

The first act appeared to be over. The actors had quit the stage, and the orchestra had taken their seats. She frowned. No wonder the audience was confused. It had to be time for intermission, but the curtains had not been closed. Something unexpected was happening.

The theatre manager walked onstage and motioned one of the violinists up from the orchestra pit.

Scattered applause rose above the murmurs. Perhaps they were being treated to a solo by a rising star. Jane leaned forward eagerly as the violinist began to draw his bow across the strings. The melody was low and hauntingly romantic. A hush fell as every guest became transfixed by the sound.

"Ladies and gentlemen," the theatre manager called out to the crowd. "Tonight we have an un-expected public announcement from one of our most infamous heroes—Captain Xavier Grey!"

Jane's heart stopped. She couldn't think, couldn't hear, couldn't move. It was as if the world had ceased turning, and had trapped her right along with it.

There, before her eyes, Xavier strode on-stage. Not in his fine red regimentals, but in dev-astatingly rakish attire, spoiled only by a blinding proliferation of over-bright embroidered butter-flies and prancing squirrels along the hems.

She clapped a hand over her mouth in horror.

He was the most impossible man she'd ever met. And the most dashing. His black hair was freshly trimmed, and he held himself like a cap-tain. Tall, confident, and heroic.

"Miss Jane Downing," he called out, gazing straight up at their box.

She couldn't breathe. Two thousand shocked faces turned toward her in unison. Flickering light from the overhead candelabra reflected in the lenses of hundreds of opera glasses.

Her heart thundered. This couldn't be hap-pening. Her friends and brother stared at her in equal surprise.

"Miss Downing," Xavier repeated, his voice carrying in the vast silence. "I see you. I understand you. I feel your presence even when I don't have you before me. You haunt my dreams, and you haunt my days. My life is nothing without you in it."

She gripped the edges of her chair to keep from sliding out of it.

"You've stolen my heart. And my ability for rational thought. Without you, I am nothing. But with you, I become so much more than I could ever be on my own. You make me a better man."

The audience was so still, they must've been able to hear the hammering of her heart. She couldn't move.

"I love you, Jane. Now and forever. This is me, proclaiming my love from the rooftops." He flashed a wobbly grin as the melody from the violin soared softly in the background. "I want you in my arms and by my side for the rest of eternity. Come dance with me if you feel the same."

Her ears roared. Blindly, she pushed up from her seat and raced down the stairs, up onstage, and into his arms.

"I love you, too," she blurted into his chest.

The entire orchestra joined the violinist in song.

Xavier lifted her chin with his knuckle and pressed a scandalous kiss to her lips before sweeping her into a waltz.

Cheers rang out through the audience. The theatre came alive as two thousand people got to their feet at once. Shouts and whistles and raucous applause filled the air.

"Marry me," he murmured. "Let's spend the rest of our lives making our future together. You and me. Forever."

Her heart was thundering too loudly to let her draw breath. "Xavier…"

"I see you, Jane. I have you in my arms. I will never let you go." He pulled her close, his blue eyes intense. "Please let me awaken to you every morning and spend every moment thereafter giving you more reasons to stay."

"I have all my reasons." She couldn't stop smiling as he twirled her across the stage. "I love you, you daft man. I accept your offer to wake in your arms every morning. I'm yours."

A grin split his face and he claimed her mouth with a kiss. When they finally broke apart, breathless, he took her hand and lifted their arms in the air.

He turned toward the crowd. "City of London, meet my future bride—the incomparable Miss Jane Downing!"

The audience went wild. Their whoops and cheers shook the glass of the chandeliers. The entire theatre seemed to sparkle with magic.

Xavier swung her into his arms and lowered his lips to her ear. "One question. How determined are you to see the end of this play?"

"Not one whit," she whispered back. "If you really want to know the end, I'll recite it to you in original Greek."

"I would like that." He strode toward the exit, cuddling her to his chest. "I also have a few other ideas that might meet with your approval."

She laid her cheek against the sound of his heart. "Does one of them involve a bed?"

He kissed the top of her head. "All of them do."

"I knew I made the right choice." She held on tight.

"I love you, Jane." When he gazed down into her eyes, her heart melted. "No matter where the future is headed, I'll never let go."

Neither would she. They belonged together.

Their future was already perfect.

Epilogue

Jane held fast to her husband's arm as they inched down the corridor of his cottage. "May I remove the blindfold, please?"

"Not yet." Warm lips pressed a quick kiss to her forehead. "Wait until I unlock the door."

She couldn't stifle the quirk of her lips. Within days of their wedding, Xavier had forbidden her from entering his library. At first she had thought he'd meant to hide his erotic novels from her, even though they were now married.

Nothing could be further from the truth. He'd retrieved more than a dozen from who-knows-where and lined them up on her dressing table, bracketed by two small ivory statues: one a cherubic angel, the other a naughtily winking imp.

If the arrival of two carriages fairly bowing under the weight of her crates of books hadn't given her a hint of what he was up to, the influx of lumber and the midnight hammering would have given it away.

He was not only welcoming her into his

home, into his life. He was *sharing* it. Making his library—Xavier's private space—just as much hers as it was his. Making his home *theirs*.

Love flowed through her. Her heart warmed. There was no sense hiding the silly grin she seemed always to be wearing these past weeks. She was hopelessly, happily in love and she wanted him to know it.

She heard a *snick* as Xavier slid his key into the lock and swung open the library door.

He sunk his hands into her hair and seared her with a heated kiss. "Any last comments, my bluestocking siren, before I show you the surprise?"

Unable to keep her own secret any longer, she tugged his fingers from her hair and slid his hands to her belly. "Only that I'll have a surprise for *you* before the end of the year."

He hauled her into his arms and crushed his lips to hers. "I know."

"You *knew?*" She reached up to snatch off the blindfold… and stared in wonder at what had once been the library.

The shelves lining the walls were filled with children's books and wooden toys. The chaise longue was still before the fire—the better to read to an infant, she supposed—but the interior bookshelves had been replaced with big fluffy carpets and a large, handmade cradle with warm quilts and rocking legs for singing lullabies.

Her heart flipped. She stared up at Xavier, openmouthed.

He cleared his throat. "If you're wondering where our books are, I'm afraid most are still in the shed. I'll add bookshelves to our bedchamber next, and then we can—"

Laughing, she threw her arms about his neck and kissed him. "There's no hurry, my love. Once the baby arrives, I'll be far too busy to do much reading for a little while."

"And *before* the baby arrives"—He swung her up into his arms and turned back toward the bedchamber—"you might also be too busy to do much reading for a little while."

"Mmm. Promise?" she whispered into his neck and squealed when they tumbled onto the mattress.

She welcomed him into her arms. This was just the beginning.

Their home would be overflowing with cradles in no time.

The End

Thank You For Reading

I hope you enjoyed this story!

Sign up at http://ridley.vip for members-only freebies and exclusive discounts for 99 cents!

Liked it? Leave a review!

Reviews help readers find books that are right for them. Please consider leaving a review wherever you purchased this book, or on your favorite review site.

Let's be friends! Find Erica on:

www.EricaRidley.com
facebook.com/EricaRidley
twitter.com/EricaRidley
instagram.com/EricaRidley

In order, the *Dukes of War* books are:

The Viscount's Christmas Temptation
The Earl's Defiant Wallflower
The Captain's Bluestocking Mistress
The Major's Faux Fiancée
The Brigadier's Runaway Bride
The Duke's Accidental Wife

The *Rogues to Riches* romances are:

Lord of Chance
Lord of Pleasure
Lord of Night
Lord of Temptation
Lord of Secrets
Lord of Vice

**Other Romance Novels
by Erica Ridley:**

Too Wicked To Kiss
Too Sinful To Deny
Let It Snow
Dark Surrender
Romancing the Rogue

About the Author

Erica Ridley is a *New York Times* and *USA Today* bestselling author of historical romance novels.

In the new *Rogues to Riches* historical romance series, Cinderella stories aren't just for princesses... Sigh-worthy Regency rogues sweep strong-willed young ladies into whirlwind rags-to-riches romance with rollicking adventure.

The popular *Dukes of War* series features roguish peers and dashing war heroes who return from battle only to be thrust into the splendor and madness of Regency England.

When not reading or writing romances, Erica can be found riding camels in Africa, zip-lining through rainforests in Central America, or getting hopelessly lost in the middle of Budapest.

For more information, visit www.EricaRidley.com.

Acknowledgments

As always, I could not have written this book without the invaluable support of my critique partners. Huge thanks go out to Emma Locke, Janice Goodfellow, and Erica Monroe for their advice and encouragement, and Anne Victory for her invaluable Oops Detection.

My thanks also go to Ailish Doherty, Amy Hargate Alvis, Barbara McCarthy, Carol Kumanchik, Daliana Ferrero, Debbie McCreary, Demetra Toula Iliopoulos, Dianna Richards, Janice Rodriguez, Jenn Marner, Jenn Ryan, Kathie Spitz, Lesia Chambliss, Lisa Schmidt-Ringsby, Margie Walzel Aronowitz, Monique Daoust, Roscoe Kendall, Sheri Gerwe, Vi Brandon, and Yvonne Daniels for their support and for sharing their ideas.

I also want to thank my incredible street team (the Light-Skirts Brigade rocks!!) and all the readers in the Dukes of War facebook group. Your enthusiasm makes the romance happen.

Thank you so much!

Next in the series:

The Major's
Faux Fiancée

The Major's Faux Fiancée

When Major Bartholomew Blackpool learns the girl-next-door from his childhood will be forced into an unwanted marriage, he returns home to play her pretend beau. He figures now that he's missing a leg, a faux fiancée is the best an ex-soldier can get. He admires her pluck, but the lady deserves a whole man—and he'll ensure she gets one.

Miss Daphne Vaughan hates that crying off will destroy Major Blackpool's chances of finding a real bride. She plots to make him jilt her first. Who cares if it ruins her? She never wanted a husband anyway. But the major is equally determined that *she* break the engagement. With both of them on their worst behavior, neither expects their fake betrothal to lead to love...